MW01015713

MURDER HAS ITS WAY
(BURN BABY BURN)

Thanks Bailey,
Ron Rosewood

DISCLAIMER

This is a work of fiction. Names, characters, places and incidents either are products of the author's imagination or are used fictitiously. Any resemblance to actual events or locales or persons, living or dead, is entirely coincidental.

Warnings: Not recommended for persons under 19 years. Parental control should be exercised, as this novel deals with Adult Situations, Death, Explicit Material, Graphic Violence, Mature Content, and Violence.

Copyright © 2013 by Ron Rosewood
All rights reserved. No part of this publication may be reproduced, stored in a retrieval system, or transmitted, in any form or by any means, electronic, mechanical, photocopying, recording or otherwise, without the written prior permission of the publisher.

Rosewood, Ron 1941
Murder Has Its Way / Ron Rosewood

ISBN-13-978-1475171839
ISBN-10-1475171838

Edited by Bailley Blencowe
Published by Highway 1 Publishing
Printed and bound with www.createspace.com

Ron Rosewood

MURDER HAS ITS WAY

(BURN BABY BURN)

HIGHWAY 1 PUBLISHING

.

ACKNOWLEDGEMENTS

This Book Would Not Have Been Possible Without The Following Persons

A special thanks to my Editor, *Bailey Blencowe*, who went far beyond normal expectations to ensure the writing in this novel, would be sharp, imaginative and compelling.

Thanks to my family and friends who provide the encouragement for my writing.

Thanks to *Mystery Readers* everywhere for their support.

CHAPTER 1

M urder is a simple six-letter word M-U-R-D-E-R.
Though these six innocuous letters are easy enough to write, read, and even erase, they spell out a distasteful word. For most people, murder and the motivations of murderers for carrying out their deeds are beyond understanding.

Lena Murin, a property appraiser for the firm E.B. Taylor Investments, arrived at work. It was 10:30 a.m., on March 26, 2010. The phone on her desk rang. She glanced at the call display, the number pad displayed read, private number. Reaching over the large pile of files on her desk, she picked up the handset.

"Good morning, Lena Murin speaking, how may I help you?" She paused briefly. When there was no response. Lena repeated, "How may I help you?" Brushing her long dark hair to one side, her blue eyes scanned the modern artwork hanging on her office wall.

A muffled female voice with a German accent struggled to respond in broken English. "Do you do the appraisals on the houses?"

"Yes, I work mostly on properties for clients mortgaging property through our company, including residential properties." Lena informed the caller. "Have you filled out an application for a mortgage with us?"

"No, I want that you should have a quick look at the property first. I am in the process of as you say, of making offer. I am from the Europe. I would like to know the value before making my offer. I do not need writing on the paper, can you do this? Let us call it, how do you say it, a favor for an old friend. Can you do that Mrs. Murin?"

Lena made a mental note of the comment about a favor for an old friend, but dismissed it as just so much rhetoric from a seasoned sharp buyer. "By the way, it is Miss Murin. I didn't get your name."

Lena needed more information before promising her time to anyone. Many cases like this were unproductive. Lena learned from experience that many spontaneous clients lose interest almost as fast as their initial exuberance compelled them to act in the first instance.

"My name is Martha," the caller hesitated and then continued, "Martha Schroeder. Like I said, I am only in the town for today, so I don't have time to do this, like you say, by the book."

"Tell me Martha, who showed you the house?" Lena inquired.

"Elsa Muller, from New World Realty has the listing," was the muffled reply. "She gave me your telephone number."

Lena had done some productive networking with Elsa over the past two years. "Ok, I can make time at one o'clock today. It is not something that we normally do but give me the address and then call me back if Elsa cannot make it." She hesitated, "I have to insist, since this is a verbal valuation, that you use my estimate only for your own decision making. If you need one later for a mortgage, we have to do it properly in writing. Do you understand what I am saying?"

"Ya, sure I need a figure so I don't pay, like, too much. Good, that is very good of you. Yes, I understand. I will meet you there at one, with Mrs. Muller. The address is 53200 at the Wiltshire Avenue in the Burnaby."

Lena repeated the address, "53200 Wiltshire Ave."

"Ya, that's good okay," Martha replied.

"I will meet you there," Lena responded and hung up the phone.

Lena felt more at ease, homes in the upscale area on Wiltshire Avenue in Burnaby, ranged over the million-dollar range. "I will meet you there." Lena entered the caller's name and the nature of the call in her appointment book, along with the property address.

Lena remembered she had a luncheon date with her boyfriend, Ken Ricci. She decided to send him a text message. *Kenny, sorry I have to reschedule our lunch. I will be doing a valuation at 53200 Wiltshire Avenue for a new client. Perhaps you can meet me there at 1:45 and we can go for a late lunch in the nearby business area? Love you.*

The next two hours went swiftly by. Lena occupied her time by finalizing a couple of appraisals, and taking them downstairs to the mortgage department.

Donna Mills, the document clerk for the mortgage department, looked up from her desk and greeted Lena in an upbeat manner. "Hey Lena, how's it going? Busy day today? " Donna reached and took the files that Lena was handing her.

"Oh, I had a late start this morning, my stomach felt squeamish. I arrived late for work, not my usual pattern. Besides that, there is the normal Friday push to complete a few files." Hesitating, she added, "I did get an unusual call though." She began describing the call she had received from Martha Schroeder.

"She sounds like a typical European, pushy, selfish and demanding," Donna chuckled. "They have time for only themselves. When they want something they are extremely persistent."

"She said she only had today before leaving town." Lena shook her head adding, "She also mentioned I would be doing a favor for an old friend."

Raising her eyebrows, Donna replied, "Did you ask her what she meant by that remark?"

"No, I just considered it a lot of double-talk." Lena's face turned serious. "Now, I wonder if she actually meant she knew someone I know? I do meet many people in this business. Oh well, I will ask her about that when I meet her." Lena turned around to leave.

"Perhaps you should take someone with you," suggested Donna. "It may be the safe thing to do. In fact, the company's policy manual recommends it. See if that new guy, Robert, in the loans department might go. He seems keen on you! You met him at the Christmas party. He couldn't take his eyes off you, I'm sure he would find you thrilling." She winked.

Blushing, Lena quickly dismissed the suggestion. "Robert! Oh, no, I don't want to encourage him in even the smallest way." Lena patted her purse, "I have my cell phone handy if I need to call someone. I also have Ken meeting me there later. I'll be fine, thanks for your advice though." Turning and walking down the hallway, Lena left the building through the rear door exiting on to the parking lot.

Donna went back to her desk and began sorting through the morning mail. Glancing up and watching Lena pass by the window, a feeling of uneasiness swept over Donna. She looked down, and muttered, "I've been watching too many scary late night TV shows."

CHAPTER 2

Lena drove the twenty minutes to the Wiltshire Avenue address. She saw a middle aged, longhaired blond woman in a colorful red and white striped summer dress waiting at the curb. She was wearing dark sunglasses and carrying a large white purse. Parked across the street was a steel-gray BMW SUV with tinted windows. Lena saw the shadowy outline of a male sitting in the driver's seat. Lena parked her car on the side of the street and felt a nervous feeling come over her body; her squeamish stomach from this morning came back to her.

She decided to phone Ken. "Hi Ken, listen, I only have a moment. How far away are you? I'm on Wiltshire and things look out of place. My client is here but her partner is staying in the background and I can't see any sign of Elsa, the realtor either."

Ken looked at his watch and answered without hesitation. "I just left the service station on 12th. I'm ten minutes away, leave your cell phone on and I will monitor everything you hear and say." Ken reassured her by adding. "Don't worry honey, this is Vancouver in the middle of a spring day, you'll be fine. I'll be there soon."

Lena stepped out of the car and greeted Martha. "Mrs. Schroeder, I'm Lena how are you?" Extending her hand, Lena felt a chill as she shook Martha's cold hand. "Where is Elsa? Have you heard from her?"

Withdrawing her hand Martha answered, smiling, "I got a call a few minutes ago, and Elsa said that she was running late. She suggested that you use your lockbox key. She said she would be along in half an hour to recheck the locks." Martha smiled again, in a relaxing manner, stepping aside, signifying she was ready to follow Lena up the steps on to the front porch.

"Yes, I suppose that will work." Lena began leading the way, "Does your partner want to join us?" she enquired.

"He saw the house yesterday, but I'll check and see if he wishes to join us." Turning, Martha left.

Lena continued up the stairs on to the large porch deck. She spotted the lockbox next to the front door. Bending down she began entering her personal six-digit code into the box to gain access to the house key.

Hearing footsteps behind her, she began opening the lockbox door. "I'll have the door open in a minute." Lena commented over her shoulder without fully turning her head. Reaching into the lock box for the key, she began standing up to insert the key in the door lock.

Immediately behind her, a man's low guttural voice spoke out. "Your boyfriend says hi! "

Lena half turned gasping "Ken?" Panic gripped her as she saw a hooded dark figure crouch and lunge at her, with a knife in one hand, and a spray bottle in the other. She began to scream. A knife was being thrust deep into her mid rib cage, a searing flash of pain streaked through her body. The blade hit bone, and then slid between her middle ribs sinking deeper into her. She felt searing pain from the twisting knife.

The attacker shouted, while stabbing her repeatedly. "How does this feel, bitch? Are you enjoying it? Am I doing it right now? Does this meet with your fucking high-class standards? Will this shut you up?"

Lena began losing consciousness. Feeling three more quick vicious stabs, she sank to her knees. In the far distance, she heard Ken's voice on the cell phone in her left hand. Two hard kicks to her legs by her attacker knocked her right down, rolling her over on to her back.

"Lena, what the hell is going on over there? Is everything ok? " Ken's voice emanated from the phone.

Lena vaguely felt the cell phone wrenched from her hand. A cold spray of gasoline hit her face and began running down her clothes.

There was intense heat, as flames began engulfing her. Her bladder and colon lost control, making her urine spurt against the burning clothes, defecating completely, she slipped towards unconsciousness. The last words she heard were, "burn baby burn." She experienced a brilliant flash of white light. Then total, unyielding blackness crashed against her senses. Nothing.

Ken was driving towards Wiltshire when his hands free cell phone blared out, "Your boyfriend says hi!" Following immediately was Lena's cry of "Ken."

"What the hell, is going on there," he shouted into his headset. He heard some grunting and gasping, then a male voice presumably threatening Lena. "How does this feel, bitch? Are you enjoying it? Am I doing it the right way now? Does this meet with your fucking high-class standards? Will this shut you up?"

A man's voice emanated from the phone, "burn baby burn." Ken heard two thuds resembling the sound of a sack of potatoes being dropped, followed by running footsteps. A few seconds later, he heard a vehicle speeding away to the sound of peeling rubber. Ken noticed a BMW SUV flashing by him going in the opposite direction. The vehicle's license plates were covered by mud.

On his cell phone, he heard a woman's voice blare. "Maurice, are you sure the bitch is dead?" After a short pause, he heard her add, "We can't afford to make it the mistake!"

"There you go with your stupid questions. Shut the fuck up Steffi and drive! Believe me it's done! Christ himself couldn't bring back that self-righteous bitch. Now, keep your Goddamn speed down to normal, will you? Go north on the Grandview highway just ahead."

There was a pause, then Ken heard the man exclaim "This God damn phone is on!" followed by a sudden *click* as it was turned off.

The phone went dead. Ken tried to redial Lena's phone, but it went straight to voicemail. He quickly dialed 911.

"911, what is your emergency?"

Ken shouted, "There's a dark grey four door BMW SUV driving

north on the Grandview just past Willington. I'm sure they're leaving the scene of a crime."

"What kind of crime?"

"I think my girlfriend has been attacked, she is attending an appointment in Burnaby. The address is 53200 Wiltshire." He continued detailing the information he had gleaned from talking to Lena as well as what he had heard by listening to Lena's cell phone. "Call an ambulance please. I'm within a minute of the house." Ken ended the call.

Ken saw Lena's car parked further up the Avenue. He pulled up behind Lena's car, jumped out of his car and ran up the sidewalk to the front porch. Lena's twisted smoldering body was lying in a half-fetal position. Ken drew a deep breath and fell to his knees.

The smell of gas fumes and charred clothes filled the air. Lena was curled up on the porch deck. Blood was oozing from her clothing and dripping down between the floor planks next to her body. Kneeling beside her, Ken turned her over from her side to her back. Lifting her head, he checked for any signs of life. He realized there wasn't anything to be done. He held her close moaning, "Lena, oh my Lena!"

The sound of sirens signaled the arrival of a nearby police cruiser, followed by an ambulance that had been dispatched to the address. Two uniformed officers exited their car, drew their guns and began approaching the house. Ken placed Lena's body on to the ground and slowly stood up, "Hold it fellow," warned one of the police officers signaling Ken to raise his arms. The other police officer was radioing for backup units. As they surveyed the scene, the policemen showed astonishment on their faces. This was a prestigious area and crimes like these were not the norm for this neighborhood. "Call the serious crime unit down here," the first officer commanded.

Ken was shaken back to reality. Still looking down at Lena, he stood up raising his arms. Realizing he was going to be questioned by the investigators, thoughts flashed through his mind. *Should I tell them everything I heard? What about the phrase, 'Your boyfriend says hi?' I was Lena's boyfriend. Will that make me the main suspect? Should I talk to a lawyer first?* A thousand things flashed through his mind. He stood frozen to the spot, unable to move.

The policeman put a hand on Ken's left shoulder and beckoned with his free hand for Ken to move away from the body. Patting Ken down to insure he possessed no weapons, he took Ken's cell phone.

"Sir, you will have to wait in the cruiser until the serious crime unit arrives." They walked the short distance to the cruiser.

A small curious crowd of passers-by began to gather a few feet away. Ken obligingly stepped into the cruiser and away from the prying eyes of the onlookers. He hoped some of them had seen him drive up to the house after the other car had raced away. That would go a long way in establishing his innocence.

Sergeant Rodney Blair, a fifteen-year veteran with the RCMP, arrived a half hour later. The crime scene had been secured with yellow tape and a constable with a login sheet on a clipboard stood guard at the only entry at the top of the porch. Signing in and listing his badge number, Rod noticed the signature of his partner Corporal Brian Smith, and the first responders, they were the only ones on the scene. Corporal Smith turned with a notepad in his hand. He looked up and stepped aside, allowing Rod to get the full impact of the scene.

The recognizable smell of death permeated the still afternoon air. The air was filled with the scent of blood and tissue, much like that of a butcher shop. A copper like odor wafted up from the body combined with the stench of gas fumes, urine and defecated material.

Corporal Smith reported. "Indications are the victim was stabbed several times and then lit up."

"We'll let the Coroner confirm that. Is there any sign of the murder weapon, gas containers or related items?" Rod asked.

"There is a .49 cent Bic lighter; however the container that held the accelerant is still missing. I'm waiting for forensics on the lighter."

"Have you questioned the onlookers out there as to what they saw if anything?" Rod enquired.

"No one came forward other than the first person on the street. He remarked that the police car sirens made him step out of his house. He is a shift worker and was woken when he heard the sirens."

"Let's you and I knock on a few doors, you go two blocks east and I'll go west. Let's see if anyone recalls anything unusual."

Leaving the scene, they began canvassing the neighborhood.

CHAPTER 3

Len Marks sipped his coffee as the morning sun filtered through his breakfast nook window. He had a satisfied look on his face. His publisher had just accepted his eighth murder mystery book, *Murder on 41st Avenue.* Nine months of researching, outlining, writing, rewriting, and cover designing was finally paying off. He had celebrated by taking an afternoon drive to Whistler Mountain Ski Resort where he spent the day skiing and the evening lounging in the sports bar.

It was time to consider taking some well-deserved rest before starting his next novel. Being a retired psychologist, he worked occasionally with the area's RCMP investigators, often testifying in court as an expert witness for Crown prosecutors. If ever there was an expert person on the psychology of a murderer, Len was that man.

Opening the morning edition of the Vancouver Sun, Len spotted the screaming headline. *Former Beauty Queen Murdered!* A file picture from three years earlier showed Lena Murin, a dark haired, young woman, with a Miss Calgary Stampede 2007 banner diagonally enhancing her torso. Len recalled attending the pageant, his niece from Calgary had been a contestant and runner up in the Miss Junior competition. He remembered Lena Murin, and the impact she had on the spectators including her fellow contestants. Everyone began clapping when the standout choice, Lena, was the judges' choice. Rallying around her the other contestants showered Lena with congratulatory well wishes.

Len wondered what events had transpired during the past two years that led to the tragic death of this former beauty queen. He began reading the article. The police investigation was in the early stages. As is the practice, extremely few details were being made public. The police were appealing to the public to come forward with any pertinent information that would assist them in solving the case.

Speculating about the motive for this murder, Len thought for a moment. *There was always a motive.* That was an understood fact. Motive was the key to solving most crimes. Through his experience from studying real cases and in his writing of crime novels, motivation was the key. Many of his novels were patterned after real life cases and motive always appeared to be, money, passion, jealousy, revenge, mental illness, or gang vengeance. Deciding to follow the news releases, as they developed in the following days and weeks, Len saved a clipping of the news story.

Len had an in with the serious crime investigation unit of the RCMP, Sergeant Rodney Blair. Len used Rodney as a consultant on investigative procedures included in his novels. He knew better than to expect to receive any juicy inside information from Rod. However, Len could possibly get a feel for how the case was proceeding. Much could be gleaned by carefully noting the tone and attitude of police officers when answering queries. Often what they did not say was more important than what they did say. He would call Rod in a couple of days.

After being finger printed, Ken spent a restless night in the Burnaby RCMP lockup. He had requested a lawyer and avoided answering any questions from the police about Lena's murder. By refusing to talk, he was informed that they were holding him as a person of interest. The interrogating would begin when he had legal counsel present, assuming his lawyer thought it prudent to cooperate with the investigators.

Contemplating the events of the past eighteen hours, his normal happy life was turning into a horror story. Lena was dead. He was considered a possible suspect. So far, he had no solid alibi prior to arriving on the scene. Everything was contingent on him explaining what happened in those brief minutes before Lena's murder.

His mind went over the details of Lena's activities during the past two months he had known her. They had been spending a fair amount of time together since they began dating and had shared many details of their past with each other. Ken was hoping to uncover some minute fact that might have a bearing on the killer's motive. There had to be something tangible that would help the investigators, perhaps pointing to a possible suspect or person. Obviously, there had to be someone who knew more about Lena and her past than he did.

CHAPTER 4

Lena had been born and raised in Toronto and graduated with a Commerce degree from the University of Toronto. Subsequently, she took two more years of study in property appraisal, qualifying her as a mortgage specialist.

Lena's first position had been in Calgary with Wild Rose Investments. It was a small, new, aggressive firm, which was financed in part by offshore money. Ken remembered that Lena had made several business trips to the Bahamas and Jamaica. Those trips involved financing of multimillion dollar commercial and apartment property acquisitions. The properties were located in all major Canadian cities such as, Vancouver, Victoria, Calgary, Montreal and Toronto. In many cases, she began to notice that her superiors were often approving amounts larger than were warranted by her appraisal information.

Lena had sensed money-laundering activities were involved and she began to look at alternative employment opportunities. Deciding to join a more mainstream employer, she ended up taking a position with Devonshire Investments in Calgary which confined its' business dealings to Western Canadian projects. During the next two years she built a solid reputation with lending institutions as a fair-minded hardworking individual. Her files and reports were clear and accurate and in short order, she became the assistant to the vice president. Her career appeared to be fast tracking up the corporate ranks and would soon become a success story.

With Less travel, it was possible for Lena to enjoy a more normal personal life. She finally had time for a social life. Randy Romanov, a college chum from Toronto, had moved to Calgary.

The two, who had been one-time lovers, resumed their passion for each other.

Randy, was a tall, dark, muscular, well-dressed young man and very articulate. He was a skillful negotiator, and had several positions with workers' unions in both Toronto and in Ottawa. Calgary was not as kind to hard-nosed union organizers and Randy was finding it difficult to obtain a steady position. However, wanting to remain near Lena, Randy free-lanced as a consultant. His clients were unions that were in the throes of an employer conflict. In many cases, he was able to make suggestions that broke deadlocks. He was both revered and feared, as he offered practical, but less than ideal, solutions and not false hope to those that retained his services.

Randy gradually found himself compromising ethical negotiations by using strong arming tactics. To that end, he had a few contacts with underworld connections that were glad to provide a little muscle, intimidating company negotiators into seeing issues more clearly. These favors came at a price, and Randy found himself being drawn into the illegal drug trade. He quickly saw the opportunity to use his high profile status to safely transport drugs and reap tidy profits.

Lena broke off the relationship with Randy in late 2007, when she learned of his drug-dealing sideline, after he was charged with possession. Randy was able to beat the charge when the case was dismissed based on an illegal search. That still made Lena uncomfortable.

She left for Vancouver two weeks later, in spite of verbal threats from Randy. In fact, on a recent return visit to Calgary, her sister's property owner had to give Randy a warning when he dropped by demanding to speak with Lena.

Ken thought that the police would be interested in talking to Randy, making a mental note to be certain to mention Lena's brief involvement with Randy.

CHAPTER 5

Rod Blair arrived at the Burnaby police detachment in mid-morning. On the previous afternoon, he had authorized a police guard on the Lena's apartment. He planned to go by the apartment later in the afternoon.

Rod had visited the crime scene again earlier that morning and had a preliminary discussion with the remaining crime scene personnel and the coroner. For a second time he studied the attending officer's report on his desk. The pictures of the victim and the crime scene were in order, however the details in the report were few and the motive was still in doubt. Perhaps the victim's boyfriend would provide some solid information on the case, when his lawyer finally arrived at the station. He requested Ken to be brought up to the interview room at ten o'clock.

The inquiries Rod and Corporal Smith made near the crime scene hadn't uncovered anything helpful. He instructed his investigators to expand their door-to-door canvass of the Wiltshire area for possible witnesses. Since no other calls were made to 911, Rod was skeptical whether anyone saw or heard anything. It appeared doubtful if a license plate number or descriptions of people or vehicles in the area would be obtained.

Rod wandered down the hall to the lunchroom for coffee, he needed to keep his wits and stay alert, the early days of a case were the most prominent and he was impatient to start interviewing people connected to the case. The first two days would be critical in establishing credible details from any possible witnesses as to the comings and goings in the neighborhood. He called E.B.Taylor Investments and spoke to the manager Mr.

Brock. Rod planned to head there on his way back to the crime scene that afternoon. Mr. Brock confirmed that Lena's friend Donna, the last person in the office Lena spoke with on Friday afternoon, would be there.

⌖

Arnie Silverman, criminal defense lawyer, met briefly with Ken prior to accompanying him to the main interrogation room. Ken described to him in detail the events of the previous afternoon to Arnie.

Arnie offered him straightforward advice, "Ken, I would advise you to cooperate fully with the investigating officers. Confine your comments to the things you know or heard for certain. Do not speculate or give excuses on any aspect of the case. If you get a question that you may not know how to answer, I will be there to advise you. It is that simple, if anything can be called simple. You did not commit this crime, and therefore you are an important source of help to the police. Now let's go meet with them. Is there anything that is not clear in what I just told you?"

Ken shook his head. "Will I be free to go after the questioning?"

"I don't see why not! Nevertheless, that will be determined by the police, after they have your statement."

⌖

"I'm Sergeant Blair" Rod said as he extended his hand first to Ken then to Arnie. He had met Arnie before. "Take a seat gentleman," he paused turning on a recording machine. "With your permission I will record everything we say on audio tape."

Arnie nodded "Fine by us, I will need a copy of the tape for my records."

"Now, Mr. Ricci, I understand that you were Miss Murrin's man-friend?"

"Yes, I have known her for approximately two months, we met early in February."

"When did you last see her alive?" Rod paused," I'm sorry to be so blunt."

"I understand it's your job sir. I saw her in person last Sunday. We spent the afternoon at Stanley Park and then had takeout at her apartment. I left the next morning."

"And on the day of the murder, how did you come to be at the scene so quickly?"

"I had a lunch appointment to meet her at 1:30. She phoned me on her cell when she became nervous with her prospective clients. I had just finished refueling my car."

"Did you keep the receipt?"

"No! I wish I had. My debit card should show the date and place though. It was near Rupert and Broadway."

"That should enable us to determine the date and exact time." Rod changed the line of questioning. "Now referring back to Lena, I understand she was on an appraisal assignment?"

"Yes, her office may know more about that, it was a rush job of some sort."

"You say she became nervous? What exactly did she say?"

"She indicated that things looked out of place, and the realtor, Elsa, had not shown for the meeting. We decided to leave our cell phones turned on until I arrived."

"Elsa? Do you know her last name?"

"No, she's the listing agent on the property. Her sign is on the lawn of the property. Lena's office may know."

"Just a second," Rod looked down, "it's here in the report, Elsa Mueller. Good I will be contacting her this afternoon. Now getting back to the cell phone data, what did you actually hear after her initial call to you?"

"Yes, she left the phone on." Ken seemed nervous and agitated as he continued, "a male voice said 'your boyfriend says hi'."

Rod made notes "What did you hear next?"

"I heard Lena yell 'Ken' and then a few seconds later there was a male voicing a bunch of female hate remarks. "Ken paused and took a deep breath. "And then the male voice finally said 'burn baby burn'. After that I heard footsteps running, a vehicle starting up and tearing out of there. Shortly after that, a man and a woman were talking. He was referred to as Maurice and her as Steffi. At that point the cell phone died. I guess when they realized that it was still on."

"Can you recall any of the female hate remarks you referred to?"

"Something like 'Does this meet with your fucking high-class standards?' and 'Will this shut you up? And a couple of others I can't recall.'"

"What else did you do or see?"

"Their car passed me going in the opposite direction."

"Can you describe it? Did you get a license number?"

"It was a dark grey BMW X1 SUV; it looked very new, the plates were soiled and unreadable."

"Was the car muddy as well?"

"No, the car was shiny, new looking."

"They may have done it to hide the number. What did you do then?"

"I called 911. Then I drove up to the house and found Lena and within a couple of minutes your men were there."

"Okay, that covers yesterday, now, can you tell me anything that would shed light on who else would have a reason to harm Lena. What about the boyfriend quotation?"

"All I know is that she had a boyfriend in Calgary who was agitated when she broke up with him about two years ago."

"Do you have a name?"

"Randy, is all I know. Lena's sister, Marcy in Calgary could give you more information about him."

"Do the names Maurice or Steffi mean anything to you?" Rod noticed Ken's posture stiffen.

"Other than hearing them yesterday, no, I don't know anyone by those names." Ken's eyes began tearing up.

Waiting a moment, Rod pretended to review his file. "Who did Lena work for in Calgary?"

"She worked for two firms, first Wild Rose Investments, then Devonshire Investments."

"Did she indicate any problems there?"

"She left Wild Rose because she thought some of the principals were not entirely model citizens."

"Why would she think that?"

"I'm not sure, I think she suspected money laundering, but I don't know anything more."

"Okay Ken, we will need you to remain here until your statement is typed up. Once you have signed it, you will be free to go. Make yourself available in case we have more questions for you in a day or two."

Arnie spoke briefly to Ken "I'll return around three o'clock and we will go over the statement with you before you sign it."

Ken, looking downcast, nodded as he was escorted from the room by a policeman.

CHAPTER 6

Rod was satisfied with the detailed information he had gleaned from Ken. He felt that after he had spoken to people at Lena's firm and followed up on the Calgary leads, he would have a good framework of the victim's past.

Rod arrived at E.B.Taylor Investments before one o'clock. Mr. Brock, the manager, opened the door to Lena's office, allowing him to inspect her office and desk. The only item of interest was Lena's appointment book. Rod obtained permission to take it with him as possible evidence. Mr. Brock also gave him a personnel file on Lena, including reference letters, educational certificates and other pertinent data.

Rod questioned Mr. Brock, "What sort of employee was Lena?"

"Lena was absolutely first class!" Mr. Brock confirmed. "She was a highly motivated young woman. She has been with us just over a year. Things looked promising for her career, we are all so saddened at losing Lena, and in such a distasteful way" Mr. Brock said as he looked towards the floor.

"Do you know anything about her personal life, boyfriends and other activities?"

"I met Ken once. He seemed to be very attentive towards Lena. That was about a month ago at a spring social the company hosted for the employees and their partners. I know she liked to dance and spoke frequently of concerts she attended. I really don't have much else to tell you." Out of habit, he looked at his watch.

Rod began to stand up. "Thanks for your time, here is my card, call me if something else comes to mind. May I talk to Donna now?"

"Certainly, I will grab her for you, she is very grief stricken over losing Lena. They were close friends. You can use this office and the phone if you need to. I will send Donna in to see you." He hurried out the door. Rod could hear him instructing Donna to enter the office.

A sad-faced young woman entered. "Hi, I'm Donna Wright."

"I'm Sergeant Blair. I'm sorry I have to talk to you so soon after Lena's death." He hesitated. "I have just a few questions for you." He smiled to make her relax. "Miss Wright, what can you tell me about that appointment Lena had out in Burnaby?"

"She said a woman with a European accent phoned her about doing a valuation on a property she was thinking of purchasing." Donna paused "The woman insisted and pressured Lena to go out on short notice by saying Lena would be doing a favor for a friend."

"Did Lena know what that meant?"

"No, she was puzzled about who it might be. That's what made her nervous, all that friendly talk from a complete stranger."

"How did she seem otherwise yesterday morning?"

"She said she arrived late, wasn't feeling well, an upset stomach, I think."

"Do you have any other information that may help us?"

"None I can think of at this time. Lena was well liked by both her clients and our staff. This is all very horrific and baffling." Donna held a tissue up to her face wiping away tears that formed in her eyes and began running down her pale face.

"Well, thank you Donna, for the information. Call me if you may think of anything else." Rod handed her his card. He took the liberty of using the phone in Lena's office to dial Elsa Mueller of New World Realty. He identified himself and explained his reason for calling. Elsa had heard the news report and indicated she wished to help in any way possible.

"Elsa, did you have an appointment with a Martha Schroeder yesterday at one o'clock out at your listing in Burnaby?"

"No I didn't. But I did talk on the phone to a Martha earlier that day and told her I couldn't show the property until three in the afternoon because I had a dental appointment from one until two-thirty."

"So what did she reply to that?"

"She said she would call me back later," Her voice gasped, "Oh My! I see now, she may have been just making sure no one else would be there at one o'clock. I feel so awful!"

Rod calmed his voice to try and relieve Elsa of her reaction, "Elsa, you didn't know her motivations, some people are great manipulators. That's what they do best. By the way did you show the house to anyone by that name or any other in the past week?"

"No, I personally did not show it at all, however the lockbox data may identify other realtors that may have shown the house."

"I will look into that. By the way were you close friends with Lena?"

"Friends in that we cooperated on real estate deals that I sold and she appraised. We did have lunch together about once every other month."

"Did she say much about her private life?"

"Lately, in fact three weeks ago, she talked about how well things went between her and her boyfriend Ken. She was beaming and excited when she talked about Ken and thought that they could possibly have a future together."

"That's very helpful. Did she mention any other past boy friends?"

"No, not to me, she wouldn't have considered us close enough to talk about her past relationships?"

"Quite understandable," Rod sensed there was nothing further Elsa knew. Her name was merely used as an enticement to lure Lena out to the property. "Thanks Elsa, I may call you again as our investigation proceeds."

"Anytime Sergeant." Rod hung up the phone, looked at the clock on the wall and emerged from the office. He thanked Mr. Brock for his time and the use of his office. While he drove back to the detachment a clearer picture was forming in his mind of what realities might be pertinent to the case.

CHAPTER 7

Feeling famished, Rod realized he hadn't eaten since early that morning. He grabbed a coffee and a donut from the Tim Horton's drive through on his way back to the office. After what Elsa had told Rod about Lena's fondness and expectations for Ken, he regarded Ken as a weak suspect, at least until some stronger evidence surfaced. Rod walked into the interrogation room where Arnie and Ken were seated waiting to sign the statement.

"You are free to go, Mr. Ricci, thank you for your cooperation," He informed Ken as the ink dried on the statement. Ken showed a signs of relief on his face; you could tell he was exhausted and trying to grieve. "I'll give you a lift home," Arnie said to Ken and they left the police detachment.

Rod added Ken's statement along with his newly made notes to Lena's police file. He called the Coroner's office and was informed by them that they would have their results by Monday noon.

Rod instructed his team of investigators to search the area of the Grandview highway interchange and the freeway for Lena's cell phone. It was likely that the suspects tossed it out on the side of the road. Rod thought about the knife, it must have been disposed of as well. He instructed his team to search around the vicinity of the crime scene and along the highway. If they were able to locate the weapon, it could possibly blow the case wide open. Rod remembered the BMW and wondered if it had been purchased in the Greater Vancouver area. He asked his team to contact every BMW dealership in Vancouver and surrounding suburbs and make a list of any dark grey BMW X1 that had been purchased in the past twelve months.

Rod was tired. The caffeine boost from his coffee wasn't holding up any longer and he was starting to feel antsy. While waiting for the results of the canvassing and the coroner's report, he looked pensively at the police file, pictures of Lena's body and Ken's statement. His eyes gazed over the dark black letters of statement and the quotation *"Burn Baby Burn"* jumped up at him from the bright white piece of paper lying in the police file.

Rod typed the words *burn baby burn* into his computer search engine, the first thing that came up was the title of a song by the singing group Ash. He pulled up the lyrics to the song and studied them line by line. It was a sad song of a love gone wrong, but nothing out of the ordinary, he thought. His puzzlement was that if this was a hired hit, which was suggested by the phrase *'your boyfriend says hi,* were the words *burn baby burn* also instructions by the person who authorized the hit or was it the over exuberant ranting of a charged up, crazed killer?

Rod thought long and hard about the comparison. He remembered the other derogatory remarks about females. The killer obviously undervalued women, but Rod figured he wasn't necessarily mad at Lena for something. The killer may have been venting his feelings from some other personal incident, with some other woman, on a day well before the murder day.

Rod wondered, was this was a crime of passion by a jilted lover, or was it a clever scheme to give the wrong impression to the police? He thought about the typical motives for murders and in his several years of experience as a RCMP Officer, the most likely motive in relation to Lena's murder seemed to be a relationship issue or a payback for something else connected with Lena. He pondered what could Lena have done that would result in such a violent retaliation.

Rod needed to determine how the perpetrators chose the house on Wiltshire; it was in an area of mainly families and middle to upper class people. It was likely that very few people were home during the day. Rod noted that the house was on a bit of a steep grade and no one standing on the street would not be able to see someone well, if that person was up on the porch near the front door. Being so close to the major roads of the Grandview highway and the 401 freeway the location provided for a quick getaway. There was no doubt in his mind this was a well-planned premeditated murder.

Rod called Corporal Smith and a couple of support technicians to accompany him to Lena's apartment. Rod had a feeling that there could be important information at her apartment that would give him a sense of direction in his investigation.

⋈

They arrived at 1120 Denman Street and rang up the manager of Lena's building. Rod identified himself and his team to the manager who then led them to suite 403. The manager stated that as far as he knew, Lena had very few visitors and had never complained, neither where there any complaints about Lena during the year that she had occupied the suite.

Rod stepped into the bright, immaculate and newly furnished one bedroom apartment. He saw that there were no signs of any disturbances and noticed that Lena kept things well organized in her home. Lena had a small desk tucked into the corner of her living room where a day timer lay open to Friday, March 26, 2010. Rod fumbled through the day timer looking for anything of importance in the days prior to Lena's murder. Thursday, listed a hairdresser's appointment. Wednesday had a scribbled notation, *talk to him* next to the 6:30 p.m. slot and in brackets, Rod read pizza. Rod kept shuffling further back and noticed that on March 18 in the time slot for 4:30 p.m., *Dr. McKenzie* was penciled in with the phone number 435-6666.

Rod closed the day timer and instructed the technicians to take it to the lab and dust it for fingerprints along with Lena's laptop. Rod instructed his team to do a full analysis of the computer and pull out any information or date that could be relevant to Lena's death.

There was a tray on the desk that held an assortment of paid and unpaid bills, some still in their envelopes. One envelope was postmarked Calgary and was a three-page letter from Lena's sister Marcy. He took possession of the letter to study it for pertinent information back in his office, once it was logged in as evidence.

A further look around the apartment produced nothing out of the ordinary. There were no medications in the apartment other than half a bottle of Aspirin and an old prescription of some antibiotics.

Lena's nightstand contained a few sex aids and six condoms, nothing considered unusual.

"Corporal, stay here and make a list of everything in the drawers and the nightstands and have the apartment sealed off when you are finished. Then bag everything that could contain DNA evidence, including items in the garbage. I'm heading back to the detachment to see if the crime scene team came up with anything."

"Yes sir, I'll see you in the morning." Corporal Smith replied. "I'll call you if anything else of interest turns up."

"On his way out Rod noticed two pairs of men's shoes on the front closet floor. They appeared to be two different sizes. One pair was size 9 the other size 11 1/2. He recalled that Ken's stature of perhaps 5'8" would probably make him the owner of the size 9 shoes. Who owned the other pair? That would be something to investigate. "Corporal, have these two pair of men's' shoes dusted and packaged for the lab."

"Roger." was the Corporal's answer from the bedroom where he was busy inventorying items.

Rod was elated with the way things were progressing. He returned to his office at 4 p.m. to the smiles of some of the search investigators. The team lead came forward and began to brief Rod, "Sergeant, we have good news for you, we found the spray bottle and another 'Bic 'lighter. The lab is processing them right now. The details and photos are on your desk."

"And the victim's cell phone? Any luck in locating it?"

"The others are still out there with the dogs, we haven't heard anything from them."

"Good work! Thanks men, we'll have a conference in the boardroom at 1 p.m. Monday. We should have the autopsy report by then. I want you all here, whether it's your day off or not."

CHAPTER 8

Rod drove home, it had been an exhausting day; nevertheless it was a day in which he felt they had finally made some progress in the case. He took the letter from Lena's sister home with him, planning on preparing some questions to ask Marcy tomorrow morning. Upon entering his modest two-bedroom townhouse on the Burnaby-Vancouver border, he noticed his answering machine flashing. He threw his keys into the clay dish that sat on the side table next to the front door and pressed the play key on his answering machine.

"This Is Len Marks, Rod. I guess you are up to your armpits in the Murin case. If you have time call me 874-2149. Thanks."

Rod glanced at his watch, then dialed the number and in turn got Len's answering machine. "Hi Len, I got your message. Yes I am extremely busy. Listen I will call you in about a week once things settle down a bit. Maybe we can have dinner out at Monty's Sports Bar. I'll phone you a day before." Monty's Sports bar was a popular middle age men's hang out in the northeast part of Burnaby, just past the Hastings park racetrack. Rod and Len had met there on several occasions to bullshit about the latest investigations.

Rod had a quick sandwich of cold leftover chicken and two shots of Hennigan's Scotch over ice. Then he began studying the letter Lena had received from Marcy, dated March 14.

March 14, 2010

Hi sis.

I got your letter a few days ago and was glad to hear you and Ken are hitting it off. Not much has happened here, Dad is still busy flogging real estate projects to major investors. Since mom died he works 15-hour days, I guess it's his way of coping with her sudden passing.

I try to get him over for a meal once a week. Sometimes he makes it and other times he is late, saying he is busy at work. Even when he comes, he eats and then hurries off. I think he knows that he has caused us problems during those pre- teen years.

Another thing, he is always cautioning me to keep my door locked and not open it to strangers. God! I'm twenty-nine years old and in better shape than he is. This thing with mom has him seeing danger lurking in every nook and cranny.

As far as your problem is concerned, I would suggest you talk to Ken first and get it all out on the table. Tell him about it, and then suggest he think about it, and you can discuss what is to be done the following day. If that turns negative then you have to press the other guy.

As your advisor, that's my advice. As your older sister, I would say it is lousy advice. (Ha, Ha)

Love,

Marcy

P.S. Phone me after you have your talk with him.

Rod sat and staring across the room. He thought to himself how baffling were all the incidents pertaining to this one family. *What were the circumstances of Mrs. Murrin's death? Rod wondered if this was why Lena's father seemed worried about his other family members coming to harm.* It appeared as though that was what Marcy was inferring. *What was the problem that Lena had to discuss?* It seemed to involve Ken and someone else. Rod looked at the postmark on the letter. It was sent from Calgary on March 15 and it had reached Vancouver on March 22. That meant it should have been received by Lena on March 23. Her pizza date with Ken was on the 24th. *Had she sprung something on him at that meeting? What was the nature of the problem that she had to discuss with Ken and did that meeting even take place?*

Rod remembered that Ken had said that he had last seen Lena on Monday morning after he had spent the night at her apartment. Either that March 24 meeting never took place or Ken was withholding information. Rod kept rolling possibilities over in his mind. *If Ken was involved, how could Lena's murder have been planned and orchestrated in less than 48 hours? No one, other than organized crime, had those kinds of connections. There must be a simple explanation as to why Ken had not mentioned the March 24 date.*

Rod put the papers back into his briefcase and switched the TV onto a rerun of Law & Order. *Cases solved in less than an hour!* That would make our job much easier he thought as he tried to relax. He especially liked the unemotional part where Lennie, the lead Cop states non-emphatically. "We're sorry for your loss, would you mind answering a few questions?" Rod knew from his fifteen years of policing that the relatives, friends and business associates of victims were rarely in any position to start answering questions.

Rod had always found it fairly easy to break the bad news to people. He himself had never been the recipient of news involving a loved one. He wondered just how he would be able to handle such a notification if and when it did happen. He dreaded to think how Ann would react. It would be a total nightmare for her to see her worst fears realized. She worried constantly about Rod's safety while they were married, and even now she struggled with the prospect of him coming to harm. This was all too much to contemplate, all these if and when scenarios made him uneasy. Deal with things when they happen used to be Rod's philosophy, and do not worry about something because it might happen. Now that philosophy was being strained.

He was looking forward to Sunday. It was his day to spend with his 14-year-old son Chris. He had planned a downhill spring skiing outing to Cypress Bowl. Chris loved going to Cypress Bowl with his dad, it was a tradition they kept up the past few years. Chris was becoming an incredible downhill skier.

On Sunday morning he arrived at his ex-wife Ann's apartment to pick up Chris and his friend Steve. Ann greeted him with open arms. There was no resentment between them about their separating. They had agreed that being a policeman's wife was not for her. They had separated five years into their marriage after Ann developed a nervous condition and had to be hospitalized.

"When you get back, stop for dinner. I'll have a roast of beef with all the trimmings." Ann smiled knowing that roast beef was Rod's favorite meal.

He nodded. "Thanks Ann that is an offer I will never refuse! We will be back around three. I'm sure all three of us will be skied out by then."

"Be careful Rod, you're not a teenager anymore." She waved goodbye as they drove off.

CHAPTER 9

Monday morning arrived. Rod was refreshed, if refreshed describes a hundred aching muscles. Skiing had made him painfully aware that keeping pace with a couple of 14 year olds, even on an intermediate ski run was strenuous work for a forty five year old. He hobbled out to his car and drove to work, grimacing with some discomfort each time he had to lift his leg to apply the brakes. He was happy it would be mainly deskwork today as he strived to piece together the Murin case.

Rod received an authorization requesting for the cell phone records from Lena's cell phone carrier. They confirmed they would be emailing the list to him within an hour. He asked for the last three months of calls and texts to and from Lena. He hoped it would help him in establishing a pattern of her activities for several weeks prior to her death.

Rod made a note to advise the phone carrier to keep Len's phone active. There had been no success in finding her cell phone. *Had the perpetrators kept it to use some other time perhaps?*

Rod wondered if possibly, Ken's interpretation of what he heard was mistaken and the sounds he heard had emanated from some other source. Rod was beginning to view Ken as a stronger suspect than he originally thought. He would re-interview Ken later today.

While waiting for the phone records Rod decided to call Lena's sister Marcy. He dialed the number he had found in Lena's Day-Timer. Offering his condolences, he calmly phrased his questions. He was interrupted by Marcy.

"Sergeant, I tried calling Lena's number a couple of hours after her death, before I had been notified. After I tried four times a man

32   RON ROSEWOOD

answered and told me to *"stop calling or you'll get carved up good the same as your friend"*, I'll tell you that shook me up."

"Oh interesting, so they may still have her cell phone." Rod pondered, noting this is why they did not find her cell phone during the search. "I'll make a note of that" Rod replied. "Marcy, we found your letter of March 14th in Lena's apartment. Are you able to tell me what problem Lena wanted to discuss with someone?"

Without hesitating Marcy replied, "She thought she was pregnant."

"Had she seen a doctor?"

"No, I believe she was going to arrange an appointment around the 18th."

Rod continued asking Marcy if she had received a follow up call from Lena after she had seen the Doctor. Marcy had not received any calls from Lena during that week. That appeared puzzling to Rod. If they were that close why hadn't there been a further communication between them on that important point?

"Do you have any information about who Lena was seeing prior to her dating Ken?"

"That was Randy, Randy Romanov. However, I thought that was over a year ago. I never cared for his attitude." Marcy became silent.

"Why not?"

"He was the typical jealous, controlling type. He would become extremely upset at the smallest thing that Lena did that was not in line with what Randy expected of her. That is the reason she moved away from here. She had her fill of Randy pushing her around"

"Did he actually physically rough her up?"

"No. All I saw was constant, loud, verbal abusive language."

"Did she mention any other men friends?"

"In January she mentioned someone from work was getting friendly towards her. I don't think she ever told me his name."

"We can look into that. Thank you, Miss Murin, you have been of great help .If you think of anything else that could help us in the case, please don't hesitate to call, again I am so sorry for your loss." Rod was preparing to end the call when Marcy continued talking.

"My father is flying over to Vancouver this afternoon. I imagine he will be coming to see you. His name is Cliff Murin."

Rod remembering the reference to the dad replied, "I understand from your letter he was concerned about some form of danger. Tell me, what was the cause of your mother's death?"

"She drowned in the backyard pool on August 29, 2009. The coroner classified it as accidental. Dad didn't believe that for a minute."

"Why?"

"Mom was fifty-nine and an excellent swimmer, she just failed to qualify for the 1976 Olympics in Montreal."

"Well, thanks again, Miss Murin. I'll be sure to discuss all that with your father."

"Man oh Man!" Rod exclaimed to himself as he put down the phone, "This case will out do *Roots* before we're done." He made several more notes in the file. Then he made his way down the hall to the lunchroom hoping no one would comment on his stiff gait. The last time he had stiffened up like this was twenty years ago while at a Cariboo guest ranch, it had taken him a week to get over a two-hour horseback ride.

When he returned to his office the e-mail from the phone company documenting Lena's calls was on his desk. He scanned it for the last call that had been to Ken. He noticed that call was eighteen minutes long and terminated at 1:25 p.m., which seemed to support the information Ken had provided as well as the 911 call made by him. Rod looked at the calls before that. There were several each day. He asked Corporal Smith to cross-reference the numbers for the past two weeks and report back to him as soon as he was done.

He noticed an incoming call to Lena's number the day after of her death, which must have been from Marcy. It lasted 18 seconds.

Rod then placed a call to Donna at E.B.Taylor Investments. "I have one more matter you may have the answer to Donna. Was there some man in your office or building that Lena was seeing?"

"Robert from loans seemed more than interested in her but I don't think anything ever happened. However, the company has a policy that discourages staff from dating. That makes some romances go underground, if you know what I mean?" She explained.

"Yes, I can see that policies can't stop people from interacting with one another. What is Robert's last name and can you give me a general description of him?"

"Sherwood is his last name. He is six feet, medium build with brown hair and brown eyes."

"That gives me the basics; keep this conversation confidential, between us for now, would you?"

"What conversation Sergeant?" She teased back.

"Thanks again Donna."

Rod found the description of Robert intriguing. He wondered if the size 11 shoes in Lena's closet belonged to Robert. Someone of that height would typically wear that larger shoe size. He ran a check on Robert Sherwood. Robert Sherwood had been issued a B.C. Drivers' license about the same time that Lena left Calgary for Vancouver. Nothing else came up other than one minor speeding infraction. He made a note to ask Robert whom he had worked for in Calgary. There seemed to be some history between Lena and Robert, something they may have kept under the radar.

He placed a call to Ken and requesting him to come in to clear up a few things. Ken agreed that he would have to come in after 8 p.m. due to a previous engagement. After Rod finished his discussion with Ken, someone knocked on his door. "It's open."

In walked the administrative clerk, holding the autopsy report. "It just arrived Sergeant!" She explained and turned and left his office.

Rod ripped the envelope open and scanned the information. The time of death was between 1:15 p.m. and 1:45p.m. That tied in with the other information. The trauma suffered consisted of seven deep knife wounds, three to the mid back area, three to the lower right ribs from behind, and one severe slash to the throat. That kind of stabbing would assume that the knife had to have a blade seven inches long with a serrated edge. Lena's body had received second-degree burns due to her clothes burning. Her face had first-degree burns from the fiery accelerant.

The internal examination report confirmed Lena was three months pregnant and there were traces of cocaine in her system. Her stomach contents indicated that she had not eaten prior to her death.

Rod added the autopsy report and a few of his conclusions to the file. He had not gleaned anything from the file other then Lena could not have stopped anywhere on her way to the Wiltshire address. Rod's intercom buzzed bringing him back to reality. "Mr. Cliff Murin wishes to see you. Shall I send him in?"

"Show him to the first interview room. I will be out to see him in a minute or two." Rod instructed. He gulped down some coffee, grabbed his files and an interview pad and walked through the general area to the interview room.

"Mr. Murin, I'm Sergeant Blair." Rod reached out his hand. "I'm in charge of the investigation into your daughter's death. My sincerest condolences."

Cliff did not step forward. Ignoring Rod's outstretched hand he looked Rod squarely in the eyes replying in an agitated, raised voice. "You can find her killer! That's what matters, isn't it?"

"Yes sir that is our goal." Rod replied in a calming tone. "Let's see if we can get some information from you that might assist us in piecing this all together?" Rod motioned him to take a seat.

Cliff slumped down into chair like someone whose body weight was overbearing. "This is too much to handle," he said in a more controlled voice. "Do you have grown up children, Sergeant? "No grown up children, I have a teenage son." Rod sat down at his desk. "However, I know what you mean, I see it all the time. The strain on the family of a murder victim is immense." Rod opened his file. "Had you had any contact with your daughter, Lena in the last month or so?"

Cliff thought a moment. "On April 2 she called me. Lena wished me a Happy Birthday." Tears filled his eyes. He presumably recalled the last words she had spoken.

"Did she mention any problems she may have been dealing with?"

"No, nothing at all, the whole conversation was upbeat. Her job was going well. Lena had a new boy friend, Ken. She had just finished redecorating her apartment, that sort of stuff. My daughter was a very self reliant type."

"Bear with me on these questions, but they have to be asked. Where you aware that she was three months pregnant? There were also traces of cocaine in her system."

Cliff was shocked and confused, then a disappointed look appeared on Cliff's face. "No, again I was not aware of her being pregnant." He broke eye contact. "I can't believe she used cocaine. I wish she had called me if she had a problem with either. Isn't that what parents are for?" He sank even lower in his chair, his eyes gazing downward at the floor.

"What do you know about the guy she previously kept company with, Randy Romanov?"

Cliff looked up, with fire in his eyes. "That jerk! I told Lena to get rid of him the first time I met him and saw his domineering attitude. After that, she must have kept him away from me. If she was into cocaine, Randy would be the most likely source."

"Do the names Maurice or Steffi mean anything to you?"

"Not a thing." Cliff again broke eye contact with Rod.

"Do you know of any other men Lena saw while she lived in Calgary?"

"Randy, her old college flame was the only guy." He snorted, "I still can't see what women see a guy like that?" he frowned.

"Now sir, your daughter Marcy thinks that you may have felt threatened when your wife died?"

"Threatened understates it!" Exclaimed Cliff, "My wife, Ruth, was murdered. That goofy coroner didn't pay enough attention to his work when he jumped to the conclusion that it was an accident."

"What makes you think it was murder Cliff?"

Cliff became silent and again broke eye contact, "If you knew my wife, Sergeant, you would come to the same conclusion. There was no way in hell that she drowned by herself."

"Again, I have to ask you, were there any threats made against you or your family prior to or subsequent to your wife's death?"

"Threats, no." Cliff looked away, then continued, "My employer,

Mid City Group and I were in the middle of a nasty lawsuit brought against us for negligence in a major real estate deal. However, it's a big step from courtroom action to murder. I don't believe there was any connection between the two incidents. What would be gained?" Again, Cliff's eyes darted to the left.

Rod noted that Cliff was not being completely straightforward in his answers.

"What was the name of the company that your firm was at odds with?"

"Devonshire Investments, they had offices in Calgary, Toronto and Jamaica."

"What is the name of Devonshire's CEO?"

"That ass's name is Steven Lee Wong. He has a large stake in the company. He's a multimillionaire, so I'm told. He even got the Order of Canada a few years ago for being a huge contributor to the Arts." Cliff added. "I understand from rumors, that he has strong political connections in Ottawa."

"Devonshire was the firm Lena worked for wasn't it?"

"Yes, before she went over to Wild Rose Investments. Wild Rose was a small, provincially incorporated company that did appraisals and financing for Devonshire, as well as other large commercial investor clients."

Rod found the connection between the two firms interesting. Had Lena, been pressured to leave the firm when the dispute between her former employer Devonshire and Mid City Group went to court?

"Do you remember the name of the officer in charge of the investigation of your wife's death? I may touch base with him to see if there may be some sort of a connection with our case here."

Cliff nodded. "His name was Jones, Mike Jones. He's at the 26th Avenue S.E station. He seemed to lose interest in the case as soon as the coroner ruled it an accident."

"And that was August 29, 2009, about two years after Lena left for Vancouver?"

"Yes, she had been gone about a year and a half."

Rod softened his tone. "How long will you be in the city Mr. Murin?"

"I'll be here at least two weeks, sorting out Lena's things. If you have any further questions or news, you can reach me at Lena's apartment. I understand I can have access to it by tomorrow morning?" Cliff asked.

"We've removed things of interest, so after I check with my staff later today it should be in order to give you clearance by tomorrow. In fact, check with us about 4 p.m. today."

'Thanks, I'll do that." Cliff stood up.

"I appreciate you coming in." Rod rose up and reached out his hand to Cliff.

Cliff accepted "Sergeant, I apologize for my pit bull attitude when I arrived."

"Hey, I understand your frustration, no apologies needed. Call me anytime you have any concerns relating to the case."

Rod immediately called the Calgary police station that Cliff had mentioned and identified himself to Sergeant Mike Jones. "I'm working the Lena Murin murder case. I understand you investigated her mother, Ruth Murrin's death? "

"Yes, I saw the news report and remembered the name from the case relating to her mother's death."

"The husband thinks there may have been foul play involved in his wife's death."

"He's still fiddling that tune, is he? At the time the coroner ruled that out, so we wrapped up the case. We found nothing to support the husband's claim."

"Did he mention the lawsuit against him and his company?"

"Yes he did. I personally talked to the lawyer bringing the action and even had a short meeting with his client. It was strictly an action for misrepresentation. In fact the Devonshire Group later recovered their monetary loss and other costs including damages from an insurance settlement from insurers that represented Mr. Murrin's company."

"That sounds pretty cut and dried."

"That was my conclusion as well. I felt sorry for the husband, but what can we do when there is no real evidence of wrongdoing? If it was foul play, it was well planned. There were no toxins of any sort detected in the tests done on Mrs. Murin."

"All right Mike, we'll leave it at that. In the event we uncover a link here, I'll get back to you as needed."

Rod hung up the phone and opened his email inbox. The report on Lena's cell phone calls was at the top of the list. Of the 79 calls, 61 had been to Ken, 10 were to her office, 2 to her doctor, 1 to her hairdresser, 4 to Domino's pizza, and 4 unidentified calls. They supported the facts so far, the doctor's appointment and the pizza take out. However, Rod wondered about the four unidentified calls, but there was no way to trace the origin of those calls. Nor were there calls made to Calgary in the two-week period preceding Lena's murder. Rod wondered if any of the unmatched calls could be the phone number for Martha Schroeder or Steffi as she was later called or anyone connected to Martha or that group.

CHAPTER 10

Ken arrived for his second interview without his lawyer. From his disheveled appearance Rod could see Ken was not doing well. "Good evening Mr. Ricci. Shall we wait for your lawyer? Have a seat." Rod sifted through his file for the sheet holding the questions he wanted to ask Ken.

"Naw, I don't need a lawyer." Ken took a seat and looked inquisitively at Rod. "How are things going Sergeant?"

"We are still gathering and sifting through information. We are making progress on some aspects of the case. In fact that is why you were asked in for this meeting." Rod looked him squarely in the eyes and held the eye contact for a full thirty seconds. He knew the standard rule of salesmanship of letting the prospect break the silence first. Even though this was not a sales pitch, the dynamics often worked as well in questioning people. It often prompted them to make a declaration.

Ken looked to his left breaking eye contact, and then quickly dropped his gaze to the ever-thickening file on Rod's desk. Appearing agitated, he replied. "Like I said, I have nothing to hide. I will be happy to co-operate in any way I can."

"Okay, Fair enough" Rod continued. "We obtained information from Lena's Day-Timer. It indicated she had an appointment with you on the 24th of May for 6:30 p.m. Lena ordered a pizza from Domino's that same evening. What can you recall about that day?"

Ken thought for a minute and shook his head. "No, that wasn't me. As I told you previously, I saw her on the preceding Monday morning, after I spent the night with her. Perhaps the 24th was a date with one of her girl friends from work?"

"The 24th memo said 'talk to him', now that indicates a man. What do you think she meant?"

"Again, I have no idea. It sounds like it was pretty important to her. If it was written like that it must have meant something." Ken leaned forward appearing anxious to learn more.

"She had seen a doctor a few days before, does that give you any ideas."

"You'll have to ask the Doctor for an answer to that." Ken replied recoiling back into his chair.

Rod quickly pressed on. "Well that's the thing Ken, we didn't have to. The post mortem examination established Lena was three months pregnant."

Rod waited while Ken seemed to be lost in thought as he processed this new information. "Are you sure? I knew her only two months and things didn't get serious until about three weeks into the relationship. I'm at a loss to help you there. In fact just believing this is difficult. Don't get me wrong, I'm sure your tests are accurate. I just can't accept all this. It's so unreal, not like Lena, at all." Ken said showing disbelief.

Rod switched topics "There was a pair of size 11 men's shoes in her closet. Do you know anything about that? Obviously they weren't yours." Ken glanced down at his shoes.

"Again I am confused. I'm a 9 1/2." He offered a possible explanation. "Maybe a previous tenant left them behind."

"You never saw them in the two months you knew her? You never had occasion to look in the front door closet?"

"Actually yes, but I never noticed any men's shoes. If they were in plain view I would have seen them."

Rod emphasized his thoughts, "They were definitely easy to spot, and they were on the right hand side of the sliding door."

"They had to be left there after Monday morning. I had my jacket hanging there Sunday night. I would have seen something like *that*. This is all telling me I didn't know Lena as well as I thought I did. What else did you find out?"

Rod ignored Ken's question. "Ken how come the only call you had with Lena after that Sunday morning didn't occur until she logged a call to you five days later on Friday morning , the day she way killed? In the previous two weeks there were 15 calls. Can you explain that difference?"

Ken glanced past Rod towards the door while considering his reply. "Well, we did have a bit of an argument."

"What about?"

"I guess I have to admit, I had seen the shoes in the closet and questioned her about them."

"Alright then, what was her reply?"

"She told me to drop the subject and leave her alone for a few days and she would clear it all up after that time."

"Why did you state otherwise, just a few minutes ago."

"I didn't want everyone to know that she may have been sleeping around."

"Let's get serious here, did you use protection when you spent nights with Lena?"

"Yes! I stayed over only two times in those two weeks, and we always used condoms."

"Do you recall how many you used in total?"

"Sure, we used three, of that I am certain. My memory is very clear on that." A smile crossed his lips. "I bought them the first day she invited me to spend the night. I left the rest of the package in her nightstand drawer."

Rod made a note on his file to indicate that since there were 18 in the original package, there were nine condoms not accounted for during that three-week period. He glanced up at Ken. "Did you not notice that there were fewer condoms left than would indicate from your described usage?"

"Sergeant, when I'm reaching for a condom, the last thing on my mind is to take a condom inventory." Ken looked away, somewhat embarrassed.

Rod reflected on his younger days. "That makes sense, I suppose." He agreed. "Getting back to your disagreement, did she give you any information about clearing that up in her call to you on Friday morning, when the lunch date was arranged?"

"No, she said she had some good news to tell me. She wouldn't say what it was when I pressed her for more details."

"Is that what she said? I *have some good news for you.*"

"Yes, I think the exact words were, 'Ken, I have some good news for you.'"

Rod stood up, "I guess that is all for now Ken, thanks for coming in. If any of today's talk triggers any new information, let me know."

Ken stood up buttoning his jacket as he slowly made his way out the door and down the hall to the front entrance. He appeared to be in deep thought as Rod saw him cross the parking lot toward his car.

Rod speculated on why Ken had lied about the shoes, did he think that it would shift the focus of the investigation from him to someone else? Rod thought it was time he had a discussion with Robert the fellow from Lena's workplace. He seemed to be involved with Lena, not only here but also perhaps previously in Calgary as well. He decided to call Lena's sister, Marcy.to see if she could shed some light on the matter.

"Marcy, this is Sergeant Blair. May I ask you a quick question?"

"Anytime, Sergeant."

"Did Lena ever mention a fellow by the name Robert Sherwood?"

"Not recently, but we both knew a Robert. In fact Lena had a couple of dates with him. He worked in the building next to Devonshire Investments. They had originally met at a nearby coffee shop."

"Do you know if they ever have a serious relationship?"

"No, not as far as I know. He was not her type. He was way too quiet, sort of a nerd."

"Well, thanks Marcy. That may help clear up some things here. I may have to talk to you again, say next Thursday."

"Anytime Sergeant, the door latch is always open."

Before leaving the office, Rod called Robert Sherwood at the offices of E.B. Taylor's. "Mr. Sherwood, this is Sergeant Blair from the RCMP, Can you please meet me at my office tomorrow morning. I have a few routine questions relating to the murder of your fellow employee Lena Murin."

A long silence was followed by Robert's nervous reply. "Yes, yes" he stuttered, "I... I... can be there at 8:30 on my way in to work, your department is up on 33rd Ave?" Is it not?"

"Yes, I'll see you there at 8:30. And thank you Mr. Sherwood."

"You….You're welcome. Good…good ni-night Sergeant."

Rod smiled to himself, as he imagined the hellish night Robert would be having as he thought about his interrogation on the following morning.

Rod locked up his files and left for home.

CHAPTER 11

Returning home that evening, to his quiet townhouse, Rod realized how much he disliked Monday nights. After a relaxing weekend with his son, he was again thrust into the hell of loneliness. He imagined that perhaps one day he might be spared the lonely experience of Monday nights and he would be able to enjoy a more normal life.

He decided a glass of wine would be an appropriate beginning to the evening, before grilling the steak that he had picked up at the local meat market. He opened a new bottle of Chilean Merlot. As he poured himself a glass, he recalled the good-natured discussions he used to have with Ann about their differing opinions on wine. Rod was always of the opinion that the $ 12 wine, such as the one from Chile, was for all practical purposes no different from the $40 French wine that she favored. Ann's opinions came from her upbringing by an upper middle class family. They had to ensure that everything they ate, drank and wore had some flair or style. That made them feel more worldly, setting them apart from the 'average people.'

While sipping his wine, his thoughts turned back to the Murin case. He could never leave a case at the office. He tried to relax , however even into the night, the case bothered him. Rod knew that time was not on his side. The longer this case dragged on, the colder it would get. He was determined not to allow this one to remain unsolved.

It was 9:30. He turned on the detective show *Murdoch* in time to see Murdoch peddling his bicycle to a murder scene. Rod enjoyed the well-scripted and fast flowing crime detecting methods that Murdoch applied to the late 1800's in Toronto

The next morning, true to his word Robert Sherwood looking somewhat unkempt, appeared at Rod's office door. "Sergeant Blair? I'm Rob, Robert Sherwood," was all he said.

"Yes, come in Mr. Sherwood, I'm pleased to meet you. Have a seat while I sort out my notes here." He deliberately took a few minutes longer, in hopes he would rattle Robert a bit more. Robert was somewhat of a nerd, as Marcy described. He had dark brown hair and a dark tinge to his skin. He was dressed in a blue collared shirt and checkered tie, you could tell he had never been shown how to knot a tie. He was nervous, but he seemed the type of person that was always nervous, no matter what situation he was facing.

Rod looked up at Robert from his notes. "Now, firstly how long did you know Lena Murin?"

"About 3 years, I first met her in Calgary. "

Rod began making notes. "How close were you?"

"Not as close I as wished, unfortunately her father took a dislike to me."

"What do you think was the problem Robert? You don't mind me calling you Robert."

"Robert's fine. I gathered he was somewhat prejudiced against me because my mother was East Indian. You see, my grandfather was with the British military in India, in the mid 1940s."

"I understand, now what prompted you to come to Vancouver at approximately the same time as Lena?"

"I came out here hoping we could rekindle a budding friendship that went sour in Calgary."

"And how did that go?"

"We were close friends, however, I can't say too much here. Our company has a policy that discourages dating between employees. Because of that we had to keep our activities private." Robert appeared nervous.

"That shouldn't have any repercussions now that she's been murdered." Rod paused. "So, you had a secret affair with Lena. Did you?"

"Yes." Robert admitted, as his eyes looked straight at Rod.

"Did you spend time at your apartment or hers?"

"We met at Lena's, never at mine. I have a roommate. I visited her perhaps once a week. We usually had pizza and watched movies."

"Now be very certain of your answer here. When did you last contact Lena either in person or by phone?"

"Well, I said 'hi' to her in the hallway just after 10 on Friday morning, the day she was attacked. She said she was running late and went straight up to her office on the second floor. I work in loans on the first floor."

"Now thinking back, when and where did you see her before that morning?"

"Let's see, I was out of town on the previous weekend in Harrison Hot Springs. My roommate and I went up there late Friday and came back Sunday afternoon. Upon arriving back about 6 p.m. I tried calling her but all I could do was leave a brief impersonal message on the answering machine."

"Do you remember what you said? Try and be precise."

"Yes, I always used the same message, except for that day. I said *Hi Lena, its Bobby. It's Sunday, give me a call when you get in, thanks.*"

"Now, that was Sunday, When did you last see her in person before that last Friday?"

"I probably saw her at the office. We saw each other there every day, unless one of us was away for the day."

"Yes I can understand that, but did you see her after work, at her apartment on Wednesday the 24th?"

Robert looked down as he considered the question. 'Yes, Wednesday was our day to meet. I saw her, and we had pizza, from Domino's."

"Did you talk about anything important? "

Robert was silent and unresponsive. Rod continued, "There was a note on her Day-Timer that said talk *to him*. Was that *him* you?"

"Yes, it may have been. We did discuss a personal matter."

"Was that personal matter, the fact that she was pregnant?"

"Yes, she told me the Doctor had said she was 14 weeks along."

"Did that shock you?"

"It sure did." He looked directly at Rod. "I was certain that I used condoms safely on every occasion. I have no explanation for it other than there was a condom failure."

"How did you feel about the fact that she may have been carrying your child?"

"I was fine with it. She was not, Lena wanted to get an abortion. She said that she would be doing just that."

"Did that anger you?"

"Not at all, nevertheless I was somewhat disappointed that she didn't want to have a child and even enter into a marriage or other living arrangement with me. But no, it was her choice and I was willing to respect her wishes." Robert began to relax.

"Did she say whether you and she would continue seeing each other?"

"Lena said she would need a couple of months apart to see how she felt about that, and after that we would discuss it again."

"Did you know she was also seeing a fellow by the name of Ken Ricci?"

"Yes, she took a few calls from a Ken while I was at her apartment. I assumed there was something developing between them during the two weeks before her death."

"Did that bother you?'

"Again, it's a no win situation to worry about it. I hoped I would be able to win her back after she had some time with him."

"What size shoes do you wear Robert?"

"Eleven 1/2. Why do you ask?" Robert seemed puzzled.

"Did you leave a pair of shoes in her closet on the weekend you went to Harrison?"

"No, I wore my sandals home that last time. We had walked in Stanley Park one afternoon. I left my shoes in my car."

"One final question Mr. Sherwood, where were you between noon and 1:30 on Friday March 26th?"

"I was in the office. I actually had lunch at my desk. Mr. Brock, my manager, joined me for some carrot cake that I had. I always brought extra for him. He's crazy about carrot cake." Robert sighed, he realized he had an alibi for the approximate time of Lena's attack. He was half an hour away, in the presence of his employer.

Rod had the same thought as he stood up. "Other than getting your fingerprints, that will be all for now Robert. We may need a signed statement from you at a later date."

"That's fine, just let me know if I can be of any further assistance." Robert shook hands with Rod before leaving with the fingerprint technician.

Noting the haste in Robert's steps, Rod smiled as Robert scooted out of sight.

Rod called, Mr. Brock, who confirmed that the carrot cake meeting lasted about fifteen minutes just around 1 p.m. Rod wondered if it was perhaps just a little too coincidental of Robert to come forward with such an memorable event, however Mr. Brock did confirm that it was almost a weekly ritual. He felt Robert was hoping for a good evaluation on his upcoming one year of service. Rod decided he had to look elsewhere for the perpetrator. He shrugged and went for coffee.

Rod spent the remainder of the day reviewing the details he had collected so far and tried to draw some connection between the people that Lena had interacted with in the past three months

Rod decided it was time to interview Randy Romanov. A check of Randy's address with the British Columbia Motor Vehicle branch records indicated that Randy owned a white, 2004 Ford Explorer and he lived at an address in East Vancouver. The suite was off Grandview, a mere 10 minutes from the crime scene. It was quite likely that Randy was familiar with the general area that Lena had been drawn into.

It was 10 a.m. Rod called and after five rings a sleepy voiced man answered, "Ya ya, R.R. here."

"Sergeant Rod Blair from the RCMP office on 33rd Avenue. Are you Randy Romanov?"

"You got him. Can you hold a moment while I visit the washroom, I just woke up."

"Sure, go ahead, nature gets the nod." Rod joked. He heard the phone set down on the nightstand with a quick clatter.

In a few minutes, he heard the toilet flushing and Randy was back on the line. "I guess you're calling about Lena."

"Yes, Mr. Romanov could you come to the Burnaby detachment and meet with me for a few minutes?"

"I really haven't got much to tell you." Randy tried to distance himself from the situation.

'What I really need is some background on Lena. I understand you and her were well acquainted for some time a few months ago."

"That was about a year and a half ago, her old man broke us up." Randy snarled.

"Yes, I interviewed Mr. Murin. Now I need to talk to you. I need everyone that knew Lena to give me his or her thoughts. Little details, even a small seemingly minute detail can break a case wide open. "

"Okay, I guess I can do that. I will be there at one o'clock this afternoon, and would you give me your name again."

"Sergeant Rod Blair. The front desk will call me when you arrive. And thanks Mr. Romanov, I'll try and keep my questions brief."

Rod ended the call and began formulating the matters that he thought Randy might have some knowledge about. After an hour of scrutinizing the file he saw that Lena's cell call record had one three-minute call to Randy's number on Thursday March 25. That was one day after her notation on the 24th about "talking to him. Rod muttered to himself, "Randy may just have something interesting to reveal after all."

CHAPTER 12

Rod met Randy at the front desk of the detachment. Randy was tall and bulky. You could tell he was a weight trainer. He had dark hair and a goatee on his tanned and worn face. The waft of last night's booze filled the entrance to the detachment. "Good afternoon Mr. Romanov, please come this way. " Rod unlatched the security gate and motioned Randy to accompany him down the hall. Randy seemed relaxed, even jovial. Rod assumed this was a work related habit that Randy had acquired from his labor negotiations.

"Have a seat Randy." Rod unlocked a file drawer, removing a file and relocking the cabinet, he sat behind his desk.

Opening the file he began, "Now, Mr. Romanov, let's start with Toronto. You knew Lena while you were both in college right?"

"Yes we spent most of the last year there together."

"And then, when she graduated and moved to Calgary, you also moved."

"Hey, I was in love, what can I say?" Randy laughed.

"How long were you steady friends in Calgary?" Rod wanted to see Randy's reaction to the direct question.

"Like I mentioned on the phone this morning, her Dad, that Cliff guy, interfered in our relationship. I guess it was about three months after I moved to Calgary. Yea, it was around Thanksgiving in 2007when Lena broke it off."

"Did that bother you?"

"Yes, I have to admit to that." He added, "I had a hard time letting her go."

"Did you keep trying to see her?"

"I guess I overdid it, finally her dad threatened to get physical

52   RON ROSEWOOD

if I didn't stop trying to see her. He was excessively intrusive in the affairs of his grown daughter. I had the impression that there was something else going on in that family."

"Like what? Did you ever ask Lena about that?"

"She said her dad had some problems, and that it was none of my concern. That was the last time her dad's problems were discussed."

Rod made a note to ask Marcy about that. He continued with his questions. "When did you come to British Columbia?"

"In mid-January of this year."

"What brought you out here?"

"I'm looking for more work in the labor negotiation field."

"How is that going, are you working now?"

"Sporadically, I just finished a two month assignment with the Longshoreman's union. I work about six months of the year, here and there, as I'm needed. I've built up a bit of a clientele, all across the country."

"Since you've been in B.C., how much contact have you had with Lena?"

"When I arrived in town, I called her. Lena said she was not interested in seeing me. She said that she had a steady boyfriend and things were serious between them." Randy's eyes dropped down looking at Rod's desktop.

"So you were never in her apartment, and you didn't see her in person since coming here."

"Her apartment? No, I've never been there."

"Did you make any other phone calls to her, besides the one in mid-January?"

"No, I didn't." Then Randy corrected himself. "Pardon me, yes we talked once near the end of March, just a few days before her attack. She called me."

"Tell me, what was that about?"

"I'm somewhat reluctant to discuss that." Randy turned serious.

"You may as well tell me now, it will come out." Rod looked directly into Randy's eyes.

"To put it discreetly, she wanted to know where she could score some cocaine. I told her I was not in contact with that crowd any longer." Randy pointed at Rod's file, "I suppose you have my rap sheet there in front of you. I have to tell you, that stuff is all old news."

Rod shrugged, "Why would she call you, rather than someone else, say her boyfriend?"

"Oh, I think she called him. In fact I remember her saying something about that, I think she said that he was extremely upset with her."

"Did she specifically mention her boyfriend by name? Are you saying her boyfriend knew about Lena's condition?"

"No I never heard her call him by name. Nevertheless, yes he knew about the pregnancy, that I know for certain. He wanted her to get an abortion right away."

Rod thought that this did not sound like Robert. It must have been someone else. "Did Lena say what she would do?" Do you know if her sister Marcy and their dad Cliff knew about the pregnancy?"

"Yes, Lena said as much, Cliff wanted her to return to Calgary, where he could help her deal with the whole thing. I'm not sure the abortion issue was discussed with them, but she said moving would mean giving up her job. She did not want to do that. She liked Vancouver and her new friends here."

"Why would she talk to you about all this?"

"I'm a good listener when I choose to be, don't forget we lived together for a year. Besides Marcy and her Dad, I knew her best. I didn't see anything unusual in that."

"Okay, let's change directions here. How well do you know that area around 53200 Wiltshire?"

"I know where it is. I have a friend that lives about two blocks east of there. I've never been on that section of the street. However, I drove by the house two days after the murder, just out of curiosity. I had to visualize how it might have happened."

"I can understand that. By the way where do you live?"

"I live nearby at 1055 Rupert, near Broadway."

Rod glanced at his sheet. "Now, one last question, where were you on March 26, the day she was attacked, between 11:30 a.m. and 2 p.m." He looked up to gauge Randy's reaction.

"That I know, I happened to be down at the Canada Revenue offices on the King George highway in Surrey. They had called me in to go over my 2008 income tax return. Mr. Nelson, the auditor can confirm that, I was there from 1 to 2 p.m., here is his number." Randy fished a card out of his wallet and held it up towards Rod.

Rod wrote down the name and number. "Thanks, that's fine I got it. That will be all for now. Call me if you think of anything else that may help us." Rod escorted him back to the front desk. There was no need to get Randy's fingerprints. Rod had them in his file from the previous drug charge against Randy.

The new information Rod had gleaned was Lena's request for cocaine, and the fact that Cliff Murin had known about his daughter being pregnant. Why had he not mentioned that fact to him? He had appeared shocked to learn of the pregnancy, when he was in to see Rod. *Why fake such emotion? What was all that about?*

There was more confusion about how Ken or was it Robert, felt about the abortion. Rod would have to re-interview them about that.

Rod called a meeting with his team of investigators. He felt that it was time to scale back the number of members on the case from twelve down to four. He spent the afternoon updating the file and determining what assignments to give the remaining men.

It was 4:30 p.m., he phoned Len Marks. They agreed to meet at Monty's bar at six.

CHAPTER 13

Wednesday evenings were rather subdued at Monty's. There was only a lopsided hockey game on the large TV screens scattered around the lounge, Pittsburg was leading Phoenix 6 to 1 in the third period.

Len was already seated at their favorite out of the way corner booth. "Hey Rod. How are things?" was his usual salutation.

Rod replied with his predictable answer "Couldn't be better." They both laughed knowing each other's responses were just so much rhetoric.

Ordering a couple of beers, Rod got serious. "This case is developing more angles than an octagon. Rod described the case details so Len would have the full picture of the case.

"Have you nailed down a motive yet?" Len took a sip of his beer.

"Several, take your pick. We have a pregnant victim, two maybe three active boyfriends, a past boyfriend, a possible drug connection, a father that's overprotective, and some seedy business operators. If it gets any hairier, I'll have to e-mail the Pope for instructions." Grinning, Rod waited for Len's reply.

"Don't expect much help from the Vatican." Len turned serious. "I think we have to do a profile on the possible perpetrator, and see which of your suspects fits the description. You mentioned the victim was pregnant, would there be a reason for anyone to get really upset about that?"

"As I mentioned the father is a bit of a hotheaded demanding person. He knew of the pregnancy and failed to mention it. However, I don't know if he had all the details. If he knew the daughter was dating someone with East Indian background that may have upset him. "

Len made an observation, "From what you told me something very upsetting caused this vicious attack or else the killer just got carried away. I have the feeling this was the work of a hired killer." He added, "I won't put too much emphasis on the pregnancy. The world is more forgiving of racial mixes these days, besides the abortion option was there. "

Len continued. "I would think that the killer could be classified as a real sadist type of person, and probably was a hit man. No one would request a killer to overdo the attack as this killer did. Usually they get the job done as quietly and efficiently as possible and get out of there."

"I think he himself may have had some relationship issues with some other woman and he vented his frustrations about that, while murdering Lena." Rod replied "It was definitely all planned in detail, until the point of the attack. Nothing has turned up so far in our efforts to locate the getaway vehicle nor were we able to trace the phone calls to Lena."

"How about the boyfriends, three you say, that by its self could create a motive."

"Usually you're right, but they all have tight alibis, only one of the three has possible connections to a hired killer. However, he is no longer close to her. They hadn't been in contact for a year and a half. He was more or less a reluctant listener, or confidant to Lena's problems. There has to be something else at play here." Rod took a long drink of his beer.

"Maybe the answer lies in Calgary, why don't I go up there and snoop around for a few days. I was thinking of going to Banff for a couple of days anyway. I can slip over to Calgary and check on the father and the previous employers Lena had there."

"Len, you're on your own on that. I can't give you any financial help from the force. " Rod cautioned. "I think that I may go up there as well and talk to some people that knew this family. The daughter Marcy and her dad are off limits to you."

"No problem, and never mind the remuneration. I need new material for my next novel. Unsolved cases like Mrs. Murrin's intrigue me. I can fictionalize it and concoct an ending to suit myself. I have a pipeline into some interesting places in Calgary. Just leave it up to Uncle Len."

"Okay, sounds good. I'll meet you in Calgary, say next Thursday evening after your ski break."

Len agreed, "I'll leave in a couple of days. I just have to arrange to get my cat looked after."

"Is that monster still terrorizing your neighborhood?" Rod laughed, thinking of the several encounters he had with Harry. Harry was a twenty-pound Maine-Coon breed, definitely a rebel since his breed was known for their gentle and loyal nature. Harry thought that he was a guard dog and acted like one every chance he got. "Has he bit anyone lately?"

"He's clammed down a few notches since you last saw him, but he still rules the apartment. I've had a few letters from the strata manager, asking me to restrain some of Harry's activities. He gave the Siamese down the hall a good licking. It had to be taken to the Vet. I had to shell out three hundred dollars to the owner for Vet costs. "

Rob chuckled. "Take him with you to Calgary, maybe he can flush out some criminals for us."

"I'd be barred from town for life if Harry got going up there." Len beckoned the waitress over and asked her for menus and another round.

CHAPTER 14

Driving home from his meeting with Len, Rod hoped that the trip to Calgary would serve a dual purpose. It would give him a clearer impression about Lena, her boyfriends, her dad and of course her sister Marcy. Rod still remembered his phone chat with Marcy, and her closing remark. *Anytime Sergeant, the door latch is always open. Maybe it's time I considered getting serious about someone.* Rod mused, as he entered the parking garage of his townhouse complex.

Checking his mail, he proceeded down the side of the row houses. His unit was second from the end, very quiet and inconspicuous, just the way he liked things. Shuffling the five or six envelopes to see if anything interesting was amongst the usual bills and junk mail he discovered, a plain 5 x 8, manila envelope with his name address and postal code, but no return address. As he opened the door and entered his unit, he placed the mail on the counter with the manila envelope on top.

Rod sat down in his favorite lazy-boy chair and turned the TV to the late news. Sitting back and tearing open the envelope, he found a business card presumably torn off a tourist brochure The *Kingsway Motor Inn* it read. It meant nothing to Rod. However, turning the card over he saw scrawled on the other side a penned message. *Do a favor for an old friend and Chris will live.*

Rod stiffened and stood upright out of his lazy-boy. Walking quickly over to his living room window, he quickly drew the drapes. He had instantly recognized the phrase *do a favor for an old friend.* Rod recalled the words Donna had repeated to him. Those were the exact words that Martha or Steffi, as she was referred to later, had spoken to Lena.

This case was getting weirder by the day. This person threat involving his family was escalating into a serious area. Rod reached for his cell phone and called Ann. "Hi Ann, how are things?"

Ann answered, "Hi Rod, things are fine. How about you, it's late and you seem hyper, are you okay?"

"Ann, tell me is Chris with you?" Rod barked.

"Well, yes, it's past eleven. He's up in his room. I suppose he's sleeping. What's this all about Rod? Should I go get him?"

"No, but I want you to run up and see if he's there. Keep me on the line, I'll explain it all to you when you come back." He heard Ann place the phone down. The two or three minutes seemed like an hour. Then he heard Ann's voice. "Yes, Rod, Chris is in his room sleeping. Now, tell me, what the hell is going on? It's not like you to be so upset."

"I received a note in the mail, threatening us. It appears to be in connection with this Lena Murin case I'm working on."

"Oh, my God, how did this happen? This is just the kind of thing I had nightmares about when we were together. How on earth did they find out about me?" She began sobbing.

"Well, as you remember, I was up there on Sunday taking the boys skiing. Someone could have followed me and nosed around the neighborhood." Rod admitted. "Listen Ann, I'm only fifteen minutes away, I'll come over and spend the night on your sofa. Then in the morning, I will discuss this with the detachment chief and decide how we will proceed. Everything will be okay Ann, I promise."

"Yes, I need you close by. Please hurry and Rod be careful."

"See you in fifteen." Rod packed his uniform and shaving things in a bag, and headed out the door.

He had tucked the note and envelope in a small briefcase. He headed west on Kingsway, taking each light on green as he maintained the correct speed. He kept checking the traffic around him and behind him, looking for any signs of anyone following him. Nothing seemed to stand out. He found a dark, parking spot about a block from Ann's building. Parking and locking the car, he hurried down an alleyway. Using his passkey on the front door, he quickly scooted into the building and up the stairs. He tapped lightly on Ann's door. "Ann, it's me he said in a low muffled voice."

He heard Ann removing the chain and sliding the deadbolt back. The door opened inward and he stepped into the apartment. Ann quickly closed and secured the door. She moved toward Rod hugging him and drawing him near. She was shaking "Thanks for coming, I'm really nervous."

Rod responded by putting an arm around her shoulders and leading her to the sofa. They both sat down. "Don't worry, we can get through this. Most of these things turn out to be groundless threats." He could only hope he was right.

"That's easy for you to say and think. However, you are here, you aren't fooling me with your assurances! You deal with this kind every day. For me it's scary."

"Here, let's make a cup of tea. Everything will be fine." Rod stood up, and walked to the kitchen area and put on the kettle. "We'll wait until morning."

"Wait is right, I won't be sleeping tonight!" Was all Ann could muster.

"Now, like I said, let's not dwell on this. I have us secure. After all, this isn't Afghanistan."

"When you're dealing with creeps, who knows what might happen!" Ann quietly shouted back.

Pouring the tea, Rod brought the two cups over to the coffee table, handing one to Ann. She had to place it down as her hands were shaking with fear. "Relax Ann, you're safe here."

"How can you say that?"

"The equalizer is right here in my bag." Rod patted the case of clothes.

"You brought your gun into the house? You know how I detest guns!"

"Believe me dear, it's needed. Would you have me throw a tea cup at an assailant?"

'Well, no. Anyway, I'm going to bed. Thanks for coming over, would you mind pulling the sofa against the hall here so you completely block access to the bedrooms?"

Rod decided to humor her. "Sure, no problem." He said as he slid the sofa into place. "There you go! How is that?"

"That'll do it, thanks, Rod, goodnight then." She smiled nervously, as she picked up her tea, turned and walked down the hall.

Finishing his tea, Rod unrolled a sleeping bag Ann had retrieved from Chris's room and he settled down for the night.

For the next hour, he went over the case trying to connect the people he had interviewed during his investigation, trying to draw even the smallest clue as to whom he had alarmed to the extent of making a threat against his family. *Who in their right mind would attempt to stop an investigation? Then is any killer in a rational state of mind? Of course not!* Rod made a mental note to phone Len and add this move by the killer or those associated with the killer to the profile of the attacker.

Rod had a feeling that this killing was not just a single, isolated incident. There had to be a connection to other crimes, cases, or underworld events that led up to the murder of Lena. Events that now threatened to reach right into the living room of his family's dwelling. Exhausted he finally fell asleep.

Five hours later, he heard his son questioning him. "Dad, what are you doing here? Why is the sofa over here?"

"Good morning son. Here let me move this out of the way." Rod stood and dragged the sofa back to its original position. "We thought there may be an intruder problem Chris, so I came over for the night."

"Who would intrude here, we have nothing of value?"

"I'll explain it all to you when your mom wakes up. Go ahead and do your morning routines, but you will be missing school today."

"Is this to do with your work Dad?" Chris was filling in the blanks.

Rod decided to confirm Chris's statement. "Yes son, there's been a threat made against us. Don't worry though we will deal with it."

"How?"

"Like I said, wait until mom comes out."

Wanting to know more, Chris turned back up the hall, "Mom, Dad wants to talk to you." He said in a raised voice.

Ann came down the hall. She too had not slept well and it showed by her tired, drained appearance. "Morning, Let's go to the kitchen table and your dad will tell us what we have to do."

Rod smiled reassuringly at the two, as he started the coffee machine. "I think it is time both of you both paid grandma a visit."

Ann objected. "But Rod, I have my job and Chris has school."

"I'm sure the bank can spare you for a week or two. Besides, the Easter break is starting this Thursday so Chris's school will hardly be affected."

Ann saw the reasoning behind Rod's suggestion." I'll phone them right away" she said.

"No, Ann, I'll do everything from the office. Stay here and pack, I'll come for you at noon and we will put you both on a plane to Penticton this afternoon." Rod got his things and went into the bathroom, emerging in a few minutes all shaved and dressed. "Stay completely off the phone unless you need to call for help." There'll be a patrol car checking the street here every fifteen minutes or so, once I can arrange that."

CHAPTER 15

Approaching his car with caution, Rod noticed it was untouched. He gingerly stuck the key in the door lock, opened the door and sat behind the wheel. His body went limp with exhaustion, though he knew he had to be strong for Ann and Chris. Before starting the motor, he surveyed the instrument panel and interior then started the engine. While the car was warming, he spoke to dispatch requesting a patrol car to do random checks of Ann's apartment block and to report any suspicious activity directly to Rod.

He phone West Jet and booked a flight, then dialed Ann's mother in Penticton, "Maureen, I'm sending Ann and Chris up to your place this afternoon. Can you put up with them for a couple of weeks?"

"Of course Rod. This is a pleasant surprise! I haven't seen them since last Thanksgiving. Is there a special reason for them coming?"

"Ann will explain it all to you when she arrives. Meet the WestJet flight 209 at 3:30 this afternoon. "

"Sure, consider it done, and Rod, take care of yourself those two need you."

"Will do, thanks Maureen."

Rod met with Staff Sergeant Miller and worked out a contingency plan in case any further threats were forthcoming. An immediate order was given to stop all public reporting on the case. They would only make one more general Announcement suggesting that the murder case was getting cold. That would perhaps partially convince the killers that the police were was pulling back their investigation. Other than that subterfuge, the case would be proceeded with as usual.

Sergeant Miller suggested, "Rod, I can reassign this case if you wish, and put you on that series of drug gang hits that have been going on."

"Not, interested Sir, I want to see this case through. By the way, I've been talking to Len Marks. We are both meeting in Calgary near the end of the week. I think we can get some new facts on the case and some relevant information about the victim and her family during the past two to three years."

"Good idea, it gets you out of town. Just be careful whose toes you step on up there. Who will be in charge of the case while you are away?"

"Corporal Brian Smith has all the information to date. I will have a meeting with him. I'll be leaving Thursday afternoon, and coming back the following Tuesday."

"Let me know of anything else you may need."

"Would you contact the Penticton detachment and explain my family's reason for being there? Here are the names and addresses of my mother-in-law and my family."

"Sure Sergeant, I have a good friend there in the top ranks. I'll call him with the details immediately."

Rod phoned his contact, Ben Walters at the Vancouver Sun and the Province. "Hey Ben, Rod from the RCMP Burnaby detachment, how about a favor?"

"Anything Sergeant, as long as it's newsworthy." He laughed.

"Run a small item on page two suggesting we are scaling back our investigation on the Murin case."

"Is that so? Why?" Ben guessed there was some other reason for the request.

"It may motivate someone who knows something to come forward with new information." Rod wasn't about to reveal his real reason.

Ben bought into the explanation. "Can I make that part of the article?"

"If it suggests that without new leads the case is getting cold fast. However, tone it down so it's your opinion not mine."

"Opinions! I have a few of those. It will be in tomorrow's Sun and Wednesday's Province."

"I owe you one Ben."

Ben chuckled "I'd say you owe me several, but who's counting? Take care now Rod."

"Thanks Ben, we'll have lunch when I break the case."

"Looking forward to it, I'm picking the restaurant."

"What no Subway? Don't get too demanding now, it spoils your country boy image." Rod ended the call.

For the next two hours Rod busied himself finalizing flight arrangements, discussing the case with Corporal Smith, and preparing for his own trip to Calgary. He thought he would make one more visit to E.B. Taylor and re-interview Donna and Robert about anything Lena may have mentioned to them in the last two weeks of her life. He would stop by there after he saw Ann and Chris off at the airport.

It was quiet around Ann's apartment building as he pulled up at the entrance. He saw them waiting in the lobby and he calmly walked over and carried their luggage out to the car. He saw a police cruiser parked about half a block up the street. The trip to the airport was unusually silent. Ann knew that nothing had changed in the past few hours so she confined her chatting to the trip.

"Was my mother surprised when you called?"

"She was most pleased, she's rolling out the carpet as we speak."

Chris interrupted. "Dad, may I go skiing when I'm up there?" he asked excitedly.

"I'm sure you can, ask the sporting goods store if there are any buses going up there. Your mother will have to go with you. Keep it to just two or three hours so you're back in Penticton before dark."

"Okay Dad, are you coming up at all?"

"I can't say, I have to go out of town for a few days. I'll phone you every couple of days."

Seeing them off, Rod felt a sense of relief as he watched the WestJet plane gain altitude and turn east. *Why didn't I take up Library Science*, he thought as he made his way back to his car.

CHAPTER 16

Rod noticed things appeared back to normal at E.B. Taylor. He walked up to the reception area. The receptionist recognizing him, smiled warmly, "Am I under arrest?" she teased.

"Be careful what you ask for," Rod grinned back. "I don't think orange coveralls would suit you." He smiled, "I have an appointment with Donna Wright."

"She's waiting for you in the boardroom. Just go down the hall. It's the second door on the right."

Walking down the hall, Rod tapped on the door of the boardroom. He heard a nervous voice, hardly louder than a whisper say "Come in."

"Miss Wright, you remember me I'm sure. How are you?" Rod walked over to the table sitting opposite to her.

"Yes, of course Sergeant Blair. Have a seat. I'm fine, if fine can describe friends of murder victims."

"It does take time. "Rod nodded in agreement, "Now, to be rather blunt, what do you know about Lena being three months pregnant?"

"Actually, I did not know anything about it until I heard a rumor circulating in the coffee room yesterday. I don't know who started it." She hesitated and continued. "I did mention to you last time that she had arrived for work late and wasn't feeling well on that Friday. However, I had no reason to give any thought as to the cause. If I had, I would have assumed she had been because of a late evening, certainly not morning sickness!"

"Would you not consider it odd that, she didn't perhaps bring that up? After all you were one of her few female friends, were you not?"

"Yes, looking back that is rather unusual. I would have liked to have known and given her advice. The topic never came up. She must have kept it secret to avoid the gossip that it may have generated if anyone found out. As you know, the staff here are cautioned about relationships. As far as I could see, she seemed to keep her personal affairs apart from her work."

"Did she have any other close friends here at work?"

"Well, Robert from the loans department was eyeing her, but again, you know our policy about dating."

"Yes, I have that information." Rod looked down at his notes. "That was the only additional matter I needed to ask you about. Thanks for your time. I'll see my way out, enjoy your lunch." Rod noticed she had two large slices of carrot cake on her serviette. It appeared as though someone else, in addition to Robert, was treating Mr. Brock to goodies.

Rod had arranged to see Robert in his office downstairs. As he proceeded down the stairs he met Mr. Brock coming up. "Good afternoon Sir." Rod greeted him with a smile.

"Hello Sergeant, did you need to see me?" He seemed somewhat embarrassed at being seen heading to the boardroom.

"No, not today Sir, I see you are rather busy. I'll call you for an appointment if the need arises."

"Good enough then, I shall continue on my way."

"Have a good afternoon." Rod smiled to himself as he saw Mr. Brock stroll down the hallway and enter the boardroom. He turned the corner and on the door to his left was a sign with Robert's name and title. He knocked and entered Robert's office.

Robert seemed somewhat surprised and Annoyed at Rod's intrusion. "How can I help you Sergeant?" he asked, as he closed the client file he had been working on. Walking to the door and closing it for privacy, he turned to face Rod.

"I have some very minor questions about Lena." Rod continued, as he took a seat.

"Sure, anything I can help you with Sergeant." Robert fidgeted with his pen.

"I'll be blunt, to what extent did Lena use cocaine or other drugs?"

Robert did not hesitate in answering. "I never saw her use any, nor did I ever consider her to be under the influence of anything other than a couple glasses of wine." Robert seemed displeased with the question. "Sergeant, Lena was a mature, straight forward, well adjusted woman."

"Did Lena ever say her reason for leaving Calgary was because of pressure from her employer to resign?"

"She mentioned some mixed up deal in Calgary but never got into details as to what it was about nor how she was involved. She was very guarded about what she said , she rarely got into specifics. Her dad was in the middle of it too! I think the matter was resolved about a year after Lena left there. She had been scheduled to testify, then the case got settled before the actual court date."

"Well, that's fine Robert, thanks for mentioning that. I'll let you get on with your work."

"I hope you get this cleared up Sergeant. As you know rumors about Lena are being circulated around the office."

"So Miss Wright tells me. That isn't unusual, people feel they have to speculate about a case like this. It makes our work more difficult to sort out rumors from pertinent facts."

Rod left E.B Taylor with the feeling that his trip to Calgary would give him a sharper understanding of the situation. Was this a business related retaliation or a personal matter relating to the pregnancy? What really happened causing the lawsuit case to be settled? Did the suspicious death of Mrs. Murin a year after Lena left have any bearing on Lena's murder? Rod thought to himself. Yes, it would be a busy few days in Calgary.

Back at his office, Rod picked up the phone to call Marcy. "Marcy, this is Sergeant Blair. I'm flying to Calgary on Thursday. Is it possible to see you on either Friday or Saturday of this week?"

"Well, on Friday I work at the bank, but Saturday should be fine. Phone me early Friday evening at home, and we'll set up a time and place."

"Thank you, Marcy, I'll do that."

"I'm looking forward to meeting you Sergeant."

"Thanks Marcy." Rod ended the call with a small smile on his face.

He began reorganizing the notes he had made after his day's work. He felt tired. It was time to call it a day. He had not gotten much sleep at Ann's. He booked out and went straight home.

CHAPTER 17

Arriving home, Rod saw the answering machine blinking. He hit the play button.

The first message was from Ann at 3:45 p. m. "Hi dear, I thought I would let you know we arrived safely. Talk to you in a day or two."

"Damn her." Muttered Rod, he was Annoyed that she had called on the landline. It could have been compromised. *At least she didn't mention Penticton.* He thought as he punched the second button.

The second message began to play. A muffled voice spoke, "Sergeant, we are most, how you say, pissed off with you," the voice was a foreign woman's accent. She continued after a pause. "I hope you said like goodbye sonny to Chris at the airport. I think you may not have, like you say, the chance to do it a next time." Then followed by about fifteen seconds of silence as though more dialogue would follow. A *click* ended the message. It was a powerful warning.

"Bitch!" Rod exclaimed, as he hung up. He was puzzled. Did these creeps actually hear Ann's message? Was it merely coincidence that the second call came in 30 minutes after the first? Did they follow him to the airport? These were not small time fiddlers. Exchanging the tape for another, he decided he would give the removed tape to forensics. Perhaps they could determine the background noises or voiceprints.

"Well, there goes another night's sleep." Rod said to himself as he dialed Len.

Len answered in his standard answering salutation. "Len Marks, here."

"Hi Len, I thought I would bring you up to date, There's been a couple of new developments." Rod described the civil law suitcase against Mr. Murin and his company, as well as the threatening calls he had just received.

Len was not surprised. "Rod, this is a more involved case than we think! There is big money talking here. I'm going to slip down to Calgary as soon as Monday and start checking the newspaper archives. I should have an informative file for you by Thursday evening when you arrive."

"I hear you Len. Keep your guard up. I think these people, may have seen us together the other night. I didn't think to check on who came and went at the bar, or to scan the area as we left."

"Don't worry buddy, I have my Sherlock Holmes hat and pipe disguise all packed. I have a greater chance of being injured on the Banff ski runs than having some low life taking me on. Don't worry about Uncle Len." That was Len's way of saying he was twenty years older than Rod.

"These are not fictional characters with ray guns, Len. They are professional killers and they don't need ray guns to take anyone out."

"I'll show them the cover of my latest novel, and ask them if they want to be the bad guys in my next one?" Len laughed, he had no fear. Len was no stranger to firearms. Unknown to Rod, Len owned a recently purchased gun, a S&W, Self Defense, SD 9mm, 16 magazine. Since he decided now to drive to Calgary he had no problems in having it nearby.

Rod gave up, "You know best Len. I'll see you on Thursday."

Rod took the trash out the back door, glancing around and surveying the area for any movement. *Why the hell are they zeroing in on me,* he thought to himself. *I'm so far from solving this case, I may be in a retirement home by the time I get it solved. He* went back inside and prepared a roast beef sandwich and poured himself two shots of scotch over ice, just the way he liked it. He just wet his lips with the scotch when the phone rang and shock the ice cubes up towards his lips. Rod glanced at the call display, it read *private number.* "Hello?" He paused, waiting for the caller to identify themselves. He was about to hang up when a woman's voice came through.

"Are you the investigating police on that Lena murder? I may have, like, something for you." The woman spoke in a German accent.

That accent caught Rod's interest. He remembered Steffi from Donna Wright's description of the cell phone talker. "Yes, I'm Sergeant Blair, what can you tell me about that case?"

"You would be surprised, Sergeant. You don't know half the story."

"I'm listening, you'd better start making sense ma'am, or we are done here." Rod walked over to the living room window and began to draw the drapes. He saw the time was 6:45 p.m. and it was getting dark outside.

Simultaneously, as he reached for the window shade drawstring the glass imploded. Rod felt a searing pain on his left side, just below his armpit, and then he heard the gunshot. A second gunshot followed. The bullet smashed into the wall above the sofa. Rod began to fall backwards, the drawstring clutched in his right hand. His fall drew the drapes shut.

Failing to regain his balance, he fell on his back onto the carpet. He lay there, on the floor. The phone handset had slipped from his left hand but lay near him. Reaching over to it with his right hand and putting it near his ear he listened to the remaining silent.

"Steffi, do you think we got him?" He heard a man's voice, then a reply, which he again assumed, was Steffi's voice.

"I'm still listening, Maurice, shut the hell up! No, I don't hear anything." After 30 seconds, Rod heard her again, "It's all quiet. I think we got him. I hear sirens. We have to go. We have the meeting with Mr. Rex." The connection terminated.

Rod could hear the police sirens wailing. Units were converging on his area. Someone had presumable already called 911. Holding a pillow firmly against his side, Rod made his way to the front door and awaited the police responders. He heard a cruiser pull up. Shortly after, there was a knock on the door.

"Police, open up," was the welcome sound.

Rod, opened the door and stepped back. Two officers entered. One searched the premises. The other stayed with Rod.

"Sergeant Blair, what happened?" The patrolman recognized Rod.

"Come in fellows. I need to sit down. I was grazed on the left side. It's burning like hell." An officer led him over to a kitchen chair. He could sit and rest his arm on the tabletop.

"Just keep holding that pillow in place. We have an emergency vehicle with medics outside waiting. I'll go out and show them in." He turned and left.

The medics rushed in with their equipment, asking Rod to lie on the gurney and bare his wound.

"The bullet appeared to have glanced off the top of your rib cage." The attendant Announced. He swabbed away some blood and applied a large compression bandage. They covered Rod with two blankets. Within minutes he was on his way to Burnaby General Emergency. *So much for a quiet evening at home,* thought Rod, as the ambulance sped down the street toward the hospital.

Two hours later, Rod was advised by the internist, that he had to stay in the wardroom. If there were no further complications by mid morning, he would be able to leave.

"Have you got a TV?" Rod joked. "I think the Canucks are playing the Anaheim Ducks tonight."

"I just saw the score halfway through the game, believe me, you don't want to see the rest of that turkey shoot!" exclaimed the internist. The Canucks' injuries make yours look like a scratch."

They both laughed at his exaggeration. "Well Doc, if it's that bad, I may take your advice." Rod replied.

Rod was wheeled up to a private room. He quickly fell into a drug-induced semi-sleep as the drip machine fed the appropriate measure of drugs into his blood vessels. He dreamt about his upbringing on a Saskatchewan farmstead. The peacefulness of the evening, frogs croaking their love songs to their mates, lulled him further and further into a deep sleep.

Murder, was no longer important. Tension was non-existent, there were no gunshots or broken glass. Peace and harmony prevailed. The prairie full moon and northern lights lit up the western night. Life was good, or so it seemed.

Back at Rod's apartment, it was 9:45 p.m. The phone rang and rang. Ann had no way of knowing why Rod was not answering. She left a message "Hi Rod, I'm worried because you failed to call. I assume you're busy, as usual, with your work. Call me in the morning. We are winding things down here for the night."

CHAPTER 18

"Good morning, Mr. Blair," was the first thing Rod heard, as he snapped out of his drug-induced sleep. He looked up to see a nurse putting up the shades on his east-facing window. The spring sun was shining through the window. The nurse turned to face Rod. "I'm Mrs. Stone, call me Brenda. How are we feeling this morning?" She said, smiling warmly.

Rod glanced at the clock on the wall, it was six a.m. "Not as perky as you. However, other than this burning in my side, and a slight headache, I must say I feel quite okay. May I get up now?"

"For a bathroom break, sure. Then I need to change your bandage. The doctor still needs to examine you. He should be along in a few minutes. Here we'll take your temperature." She stuck and clicked the measuring device into Rod's ear.

He winced at the sound as it reminded him of the gunshots and flying glass of last evening. "Sorry," he apologized.

"Hey, everyone does that." She glanced at the reading. "Everything is normal in there."

"Then, excuse me." Rod sat up. He staggered to the bathroom, still groggy from the medication."

"You won't be driving for at least six hours, Mr. Blair." Brenda cautioned him from the other room.

"Driving is the last thing on my mind." Rod shot back. He entered the bathroom. As he was washing up at the sink, he looked at his face in the mirror. His 36-hour stubble was making him look like a ranch hand just in from the cold. His eyes were bloodshot and his heart was beating rapidly.

He toweled off the water he had splashed on his face and went back into the room. "I look like hell!" he exclaimed.

"Well, you've had an evening to remember. I heard the rumors circulating around the ward." She gave him an encouraging pat on the right shoulder.

"You never can tell when a bus comes along and hits you." Rod kept things general.

"Here comes Dr. Reed now."

Rod sat down on the edge of his bed.

"Mr. Blair, I'll have you lie down while I examine your wound. Undo your night gown please." Dr. Reed undid the bandage. "That doesn't look too serious. We stitched you together last night. It looks very clean. We'll bandage you up and give you some antibiotics." Dr. Reed turned to the nurse, "re-bandage and give him a couple more for the road."

"Mr. Blair, I would suggest you refrain from doing any strenuous activity for a few days. Come back in a week, or sooner, if it gives you any discomfort. We will remove your stitches. The nurses' in emergency can do that for you."

"Does that mean I can leave this morning?" Rod replied.

"I'd say we will keep you here until about two o'clock . Then, the internist will clear you to go."

Rod was satisfied with that. The office could do without him for a day or two.

Rod phoned his strata manager Ralph, and asked him to call the glass company in to replace his window.

"I've already done that," he answered. "Their man was out measuring the window about an hour ago. I expect them back before noon with the window."

"Thanks Ralph, I'll be home in mid-afternoon."

After being supplied with a disposable razor, and having the customary scrambled eggs and toast for breakfast, Rod was resumed going over the facts of the case.

Rod began piecing together the events of the previous day. *What sort of mentality are we dealing with here? Do they think that taking out one investigator will stop the case from being investigated? If anything, that would spur on the efforts of the police to solve the case. I think Len is right, money is involved, and there is an iceberg-like piece of information hiding under the surface that we can't see.*

Rod recalled the reference to Rex that he overheard. *Could that be the person behind the murder of Lena? Was he also the one that made the attempt on his life? What was the reference to a meeting about? Were they just getting together informally, and not actually having some important meeting.*

Rod had to leave for Calgary in just under two days. He hoped to uncovering some pertinent facts there that would shed some light on his perplexing case

"Hi Sergeant."

Rod glanced up from his notes. He saw Corporal Smith, approaching his bed. "Hi Brian, come in. I've just been going over a few things I remembered from yesterday. Has anything new surfaced in the Murin case?"

"Yea, someone took a shot at the lead investigator!" Brian joked.

"I've made a note of that Brian. Tell me something I don't already know." Rod patted his side.

"Well we searched the treed ravine property across from your townhouse. We found a kid's tree house. It was high enough for a person to get a clear view of your front window. Mind you the distance was about 150 yards."

"That's no factor with a telescopic sight! What kind of rifle was used? Did you find any shell casings?"

"No, none, but the slug we dug out of the stud in your living room wall was a 223 Remington."

"That's a varmint rifle, isn't it? There are 100's of them around, especially on the prairies."

"Yes sir, they usually come with a telescopic sight that is easily accurate to 200 yards."

"If they can shoot a coyote at 200 yards, I came off lucky." Rod felt a chill traverse down his spine.

"I think the window glass may have slightly defected the bullet enough to almost miss you."

"Again this points back to the prairies. I'm getting more and more optimistic that some answers exist in Calgary. When I get back, I'll have a better handle on the facts surrounding this case." Rod struggled to his feet. "While you're here, let's get the Doc in here. He may let me go a couple of hours earlier that they said."

Brian went out to the nurses' station and put in the request." I'm here to give Rod Blair a ride, would you see if a Doctor can clear him a bit earlier?"

"I'll try Sir." The nurse spoke into an intercom "Dr. Reed please, come to station 33?" She looked past Brian to Rod. "He'll be up shortly, you can get dressed if you wish."

Rod was packing his meager belongings into a plastic bag when Dr. Reed walked in. He looked at Rod's chart. "Mr. Blair, how do you feel? Walk across the room and back."

Rod complied," I'm feeling better by the hour."

"I would say you should go home. Is there anyone there to assist you?"

"No, but I have a neighbor she's a retired nurse. I'm sure I can call on her."

"Here is a prescription for some additional antibiotics."

Rod signed out and Corporal Smith gave him a ride home. "We have extra patrols on for the next two days Sergeant. We'll pull them off after you leave for Calgary."

"Great. Thanks Brian. Would you pick me up tomorrow morning at 7:30? I need a ride to the office."

"7:30 it is then."

Rod entered his front door just as the window company was cleaning up. "Thanks for the quick service guys." Rod signed the work order and accepted his copy.

"Any time sir."

"Not anytime soon," Rod answered smiling as they left with their tools and bags of broken glass.

Rod retrieved his cell phone and called Ann. "Hi Ann, I was tied up on a late night case." He lied.

"Well, you could have called!" Ann replied.

"Yes, I suppose I could have. How are you and Chris doing?"

"Oh, he's off skiing with a busload of teens. I expect him back in about two hours. Don't worry about him. He's another you, no sense of fear."

"Okay then. I'll be going to Calgary the day after tomorrow. However, I'll keep in touch as best I can. Call the office if you need to talk to me."

"Be careful Rod," Ann could sense that something serious was in the works. She knew prying into details would only serve to upset her once again. She chose to leave things static.

Rod ordered a pizza. He leaned back on the sofa and watched the pregame show of the hockey game soon to start from Montreal. Boston was in town to tangle with the tough guy Habs.

CHAPTER 19

Len Marks cursed the slopes on Mt. Norquay. It was billed as a family ski resort but failed to take into account out of shape retired professionals. After a couple hours of skiing, he retreated to the comfort of the lodge to watch the fireplace crackle while enjoying an Irish coffee.

It was only three p.m. with only a dozen or so patrons in the lounge. Len noticed a professional looking woman, ten years his junior, saunter and stand in front of the fireplace. She shook her long dark hair after removing her blue headband. Her bright blue eyes flashed as she turned and looked around the room. It appeared she was looking for someone. She saw Len and smiled, "Sorry for blocking your view." She stepped to one side of the fireplace.

"Hey, the view was much improved with you there. Are you waiting for someone?" He enquired.

"My sister Nora, she must be still out there. I'm Shannon, we came up from Calgary yesterday morning for this mid-week special."

"Have a seat Shannon. I'm just on my way to your city, tomorrow morning in fact."

Shannon sat down in a lounge chair adjoining Len's. "I think I'll have one of those" she said as she beckoned the bartender. She nodded, and pointed to Len's drink as she held up one finger.

"You'd better be careful he doesn't misinterpret your finger motions." Len laughed.

Shannon smiled. "Oh he got that other one yesterday from my sister. He understands us very clearly now." She laughed. "Are you on business Len?"

"I'd say 50-50 I'm a retired psychologist, turned author. I'm always looking for new material."

"You won't find anything exciting near me. I work for the Calgary Herald, a pretty tame newspaper. If a dog gets run down, it's front page news." Shannon laughed. "I take classified ads all day long, nothing sinister about them!"

"Actually I intend on going through some of your archives. I'm researching a possible unsolved crime." Len raised his eyebrows to heighten her interest in the story. He hoped he wasn't saying too much. He glanced around and saw no one was near enough to notice their conversation.

Shannon was intrigued, "Which case was that?"

"Her name was Murin, a retired Olympic swimmer. She drowned in a back yard pool"

"I remember her, in fact I knew her. I took swimming lessons from her one summer at the local YMCA. That was oh, all of 15 years ago."

"Did you know her daughter Lena? She was murdered in the Burnaby area a couple of weeks ago?"

Shannon gasped. "Was that her? I heard a bit about that! I don't think it made our paper in a big way. She was just a kid when I knew her. I remember she was waiting for her mother."

"Were there any rumors about the mother's death? The coroner ruled it accidental." Len fished for information Shannon might be privy to.

"Just the usual beer parlor talk, speculation of all sorts!"

"Do you remember any of it?"

"Some thought the husband may have had a hand in it. But husbands are always the first person people turn their eyes on, the wicked spouse."

"He apparently was the one that said it could not have been accidental, because she was an excellent swimmer." Len kept prodding her to talk.

"Well, the other rumor was that the husband was mixed up with the underworld. He was some sort of high flying commercial realtor." Shannon frowned.

RON ROSEWOOD

"There are dozens of those around, I'm sure they're hardworking honest sorts, like you and I." Len smiled at the self compliment.

"True, but they can't pick their clients that carefully. Making a sale is their top priority, the buyer and the money source is secondary."

"Well, anyhow let's not let our work, spoil a nice evening. Would you and your sister join me for any early dinner? I'll be leaving for town early in the morning."

"Sure, I'd love to. We'll wait for Nora and see if she'd like to join us?"

"I'm getting another coffee, are you ready for another?" Len stood up and reached toward her mug.

"No thanks, I have plenty here. You go ahead." Shannon smiled as she spoke.

While Len was waiting at the bar, he saw a younger version of Shannon with a companion in tow approach Nora. It was obvious they were going to be spending time together. After a few minutes, the two left. Len returned to the fireplace lounge." Was that your sister?"

"That's my crazy sister, all right. Do you know what she did?" Without waiting for Len to reply she continued. "She joined up on one of those 'speed dating on a chairlift deals,' and she met that guy. They are going over to his hotel for the evening."

Len grinned. "Love at first sight, I've heard of it, but never experienced it myself."

"I think us older folks are a bit more reserved than our younger counterparts."

"That may be why we are often alone. Anyhow, that isn't the case tonight. Let's head over to the adjoining dining area and have a nice quiet old fashioned meal."

"Sure, why not" Shannon stood up and took Len's arm. "We'll show those youngsters a thing or two."

Len had no reason to disagree with Shannon. Heads turned admiring Shannon, as they made their way to a corner table. The server joined them and motioned to the candle lit table. "Will this do?" he asked.

"Perfect, thank you." Shannon beamed as Len pulled a chair out for her." Isn't this lovely?"

"As are you!" Len smiled and held his breath, while enjoying the feeling of a woman's closeness.

CHAPTER 20

Rod took advantage of his immobility to get his team together so they could brainstorm the information available.

"Okay men, now let's see what we have so far. We have the victim, Lena Murin, a skilled, high level, property appraiser. We know she had lived in Calgary, Toronto and then back in Calgary. She finally relocated here in Burnaby. She was three months pregnant at the time of her death. She had traces of cocaine in her system."

"We have an ex-boyfriend, Randy Romanov, who knew her in Toronto, then in Calgary, after she went back there. Recently he followed her to Burnaby, where he now resides. He has a rap sheet for drug dealing. He is described as a hot -headed, jealous, controlling type. He is also rumored to have used underground muscle in his jobs as a labor-union negotiator."

"We have Ken Ricci, another boyfriend, an ordinary home realtor. He's been on the scene less than three months. He appeared to be very distraught over Lena's death. He claims he was not aware of her pregnancy. He further stated he was not involved with her in that way until six weeks ago."

"We have Robert Sherwood, he works as a mortgage underwriter at the same firm as the victim. He is also a boyfriend and possibly the pending father. He says he was willing to step up and take full responsibility for Lena and the baby. In fact, any talk of abortion was not his idea. However, he said he respected her right as a woman to make the final decision about aborting. His mother was from India."

"We have her dad, Cliff Murin, he lost his wife just over a year ago, in mysterious circumstances. She was found dead, in their back yard pool. He says it was murder the coroner says it was accident. The police have agreed. He too is in the commercial real estate and project development business. He had a major law suit going against him by Devonshire Investments, until it was settled out of court. He didn't like Randy and he is said to also have race issues with non whites."

Rod continued. "Marcy, the victim's sister, is in Calgary, she had some helpful information. I will be interviewing her in depth when I'm up there later this week."

"The victim's employer, Dave Brock, is not a player. He runs a very respectable mortgage financing company. He is well thought of by his employees and his biggest sin appears to be mooching carrot cake from his employees."

"The other employees at the company are of no interest at this time. None have come forward with any pertinent information."

Rod scanned the room, all the men were thoughtfully engaged and taking notes. "Now, we have some pretty heavy players, yet to be identified. Maurice and Steffi from the murder scene are still making noises, as I just found out. They mentioned someone named Mr. Rex. Rex could be his first name or his last name. This may turn up another suspect, so keep that name in mind."

"I'm off to Calgary tomorrow and perhaps I can gather a few more details to help us. Now, anything to add to what I already covered?"

Corporal Smith spoke up, "The gun you were shot with used .223 Remington bullets. You mentioned that could indicate prairie connections."

"Yes, Corporal Smith that is another connected matter. Also, pull over any dark, out of town SUVs that have prairie plates, especially dark colored BMWs, but not necessarily that make. We may win the lottery and find a connection."

"Anything else fellows? Is there any street talk floating around in the nightclubs about this case?"

Constable North a two year rookie stepped forward. "I just may have something, not on this case itself. There is talk of a high profile investment dealer from Calgary, who has set up shop here. Apparently he has many major investors. He owns his own airplane, a yacht and he's been throwing lavish parties. He's connected to that same Company that the Victim's father was being sued by Devonshire Investments. He opened a branch office here in Vancouver six months ago. I have his name here in my notes." Constable North took a pause. "It matches the name you mentioned earlier Sergeant, Rex Trent."

Rod was intrigued, this was a key connection. "I'll have Corporal Smith assist you in discreetly checking into this Rex Trent's, background. Find out when he started in the investment business. Go through the investment Dealers' Associations both in Toronto, Calgary and here and take note of any complaints that may have been filed against him. There could well be an important connection here. Good work, Constable."

"Keep asking questions, there is more information out there. Let's get to it and wrap this thing up. It's been nearly three weeks now. We need some answers."

Rod spent another two hours making notes and reviewing facts in the case. He loaded his briefcase with essentials for his trip to Calgary. Before Corporal Smith drove him home he called Len Mark's cell phone. "Hi Len, Rod here, a new development has come up. Keep the name Rex Trent in your mind as you go through news reports. See what you can dig up on him. He has many investors here in B.C. praising him. See if he's worthy of their claims. The company he worked for in Calgary is Devonshire Investments, Apparently, he now runs a branch office here for the same Company."

As a follow up, Rod pulled the Devonshire Investments webpage on his computer.

d46e65fd-0af8-4365-9cd5-9a7f5e916453
Y2:d46e65fd-0af8-4365-9cd5-9a7f5e916453

Devonshire Investments Incorporated, was founded in 1999. It is a property investment company that provides a dynamic, diverse and rapidly growing property base. It also manages funds in mutual funds group called Devonshire Mutual Trust.

Innovative management initiatives are applied throughout the port-folio covering all property asset classes - office, retail, industrial, and leisure, including major hotel operations, some with casino operations. The company has expanded considerably since it was founded in 1999. It now has net asset values estimated at 900 million dollars. The current portfolio is spread across all major cities in Canada, including Toronto, Montreal, Winnipeg, Regina, Calgary, Edmonton, Vancouver and Victoria. We have an affiliated company, Devonshire Investments Grand Cayman, located in the Grand Cayman Islands, which manages our tax and non-Canadian operations.

Talk about big money Rod thought as he printed out the page for Corporal Smith. He was feeling more confident that this was indeed a promising lead in the case. "We'll kick a few fenders and see what falls off the truck" Rod said, as he went over the information with Corporal Smith. "Now, Brian, take me home, I've had it for today. In fact I am booking off work tomorrow. "

CHAPTER 21

Len left the Banff area early and arrived in Calgary at nine in the morning. He parked his car in the customer lot at the Calgary Herald. The building's sign reminded him of the pleasant evening he had spent with Shannon. He had promised her he would call her before he left Calgary. He walked into a rather library-like atmosphere, approached the lone reception clerk and handed her his card. "Good Morning, I'm Len Marks."

She glanced at the card, and smiled. "Yes, Mr. Marks, I've seen your books. In fact, I read one when I was on vacation in Vancouver. I rather enjoyed the action and suspense. "

"I'm always pleased to hear good positive remarks."

"Now, my name is Sandy, how may I help you Mr. Marks."

"I'd like to review some news archives between January 1, 2008 and about July 31, 2009."

"Certainly, that's fairly current, we have it all on micro- fiche on our in-house computers. Here, I'll get you started." She led him into the archives room.

Sandy showed Len the first issue of 2008, and gave him pointers on printing any item he required, as well as the procedures for advancing by issue or by topic. "Call me, if you need assistance."

"Thanks, Sandy," Len opened up his note pad and started by inserting the name "Ruth Murin" in the browser.

The three news articles covering a six week period, basically headlined *Olympic Swimmer Dead* described the death. The next news item *Coroner Rules Murin Death Accidental* produced no new information. The last article on page three read *$50,000 Reward Offered*. It dealt with Cliff Murin offering the reward for any new information on the case.

Three strikes there Len thought. There was nothing of consequential value other than Mr. Murrin's strong view that there was foul play involved by him offering a reward. *Then again, was he reinforcing his own innocence by posturing and offering rewards?* The beginnings of a novel outline began forming in Len's mind.

I wonder if anyone came forward directly to Mr. Murin with information that perhaps he didn't turn over to the police? That was a question he would pass on to Rod to ask either Marcy or Cliff.

Len did some further research on the legal case involving Cliff's firm, finding only one headline Announcing the legal action. As with most corporate legal cases, details were sketchy, but the article did mention the sum of five million dollars as the amount of the damages sought. *That may be a motive, to ensure success in something that large.* Len surmised as he ended his search. He thanked Sandy, and left the building.

He decided to sniff around some of the bars and business clubs for some street opinions. The Ranchmen's Club seemed to be a logical choice. Formed in 1891, it was the oldest Club in the city. Len's, membership in the Order of Eagles would give him admittance.

"On business, Mr. Marks?" Asked the young business manager who had been summoned over by the receptionist.

Len smiled, "A little respite from the Vancouver scene. I haven't been here since 2007."

"Enjoy your stay in Calgary." The manager returned the Eagles Membership card.

Len glanced at his watch, it was 11:30 a.m. He walked over to the formal dining room, all set up with white table clothes and contrasting upholstered blue chairs. He introduced himself to the waiter. As he was led over to a table, the waiter made a suggestion. "How would you like to meet one of our older members? Mr. Monahan is always ready to share our history with new-comers."

Len nodded in agreement. "That would be perfect, thanks for the idea."

A white bearded man sat alone at a table near the window. He had piercing dark eyes, pale lips and skin and his hand had a slight shake as he lifted his pint of Guinness to his mouth. "Mr. Monahan sir this gentleman is from Vancouver, may he join you?"

Len stepped forward, "Len Marks here, pleased to meet you." Len extended his hand.

"Steve Monahan, by all means join me, have a seat." He rose halfway out of his chair shaking Len's hand, then settled back down in his seat.

The waiter placed a menu in front of Len, and scurried off to seat another couple.

"What brings you to town?" Mr. Monahan questioned. "If I can be so blunt?"

"I'm an author, researching an unsolved case. Perhaps to base a novel on." Len said softly, leaning forward as if to suggest an element of secrecy in his mission.

"Do you mean there are unsolved cases in this city of brotherly love?" Steve replied light heartedly as he grinned.

Len, looked down at the menu replying. "You probably heard of the Ruth Murin case?"

"Yes, of course, Cliff and his company associates have been members here for years. I remember the case very well. It was ruled an accident. Cliff never believed that."

Len prompted him to continue. "Yes, I saw the offer of a reward in the archives .Was there any talk of any takers?"

"Only once, I saw Cliff in here with a stranger about two weeks after he published his ad. They had a long meeting. Quite a few pieces of paper were being handed back and forth."

"Perhaps it was a real estate matter?"

"No, this person was not your typical commercial realtor."

"What made you conclude that?"

"He seemed extremely nervous the whole time he was here, and they never came back. Those commercial deals go on for weeks. In most cases, much detail and tax planning accompanies them. I'm a retired Chartered Accountant." Steve beamed at his keen observations and sharp memory of the event.

"Can you describe that particular chap?"

"Sure, he was young, perhaps thirtyish, with a dark complexion. He had what I would say is a French accent. You know like those, French Canadian hockey players on TV in their after game interviews? He wasn't overly tall though, just average height. He had a Clint Eastwood beard, you know a stubble-type look."

"That's something to remember for my novel, a smallish mysterious stranger" Len remarked as he attempted to make light of his interest. It seemed that Steve had not heard of Lena's murder. Len would keep it that way for now.

"Well look at this menu, what would you recommend Steve?"

"The most popular item is the 8oz steak sandwich, don't forget, you're in Cowboy Country." He chuckled.

Len laughed, "This cowboy is having a steak sandwich then." They placed their orders.

Len diverted the conversation to skiing, hunting, hockey and football as they enjoyed the day exchanging opinions and experiences.

Len saw Steve as a colorful character. Perhaps he could work this character into his new novel.

CHAPTER 22

"Have a pleasant trip, Sergeant, "Corporal Smith remarked as he escorted Rod to the boarding gate.

"This may be just what I need" Rod exclaimed. "A change of scenery and some fresh country air! Although, I shouldn't describe Calgary as country." Rod took his briefcase from Brian.

"Calgaryites like to think so!" Corporal Smith extended his hand to Rod. "I'll see you in a few days."

"Keep in touch, you have my cell number." Rod remarked over his shoulder as he turned and walked toward the holding area.

Two hours later, Rod was exiting a Yellow cab at the Delta-Bow Valley Hotel in downtown Calgary. He checked in and retired to his room. Rod decided he would have a short rest before calling Len. He still felt pain in his left side from the tender wound. He removed his outerwear and relaxed as he turned on the sports channel.

Two hours later, he awoke from and glanced at his watch, 5:30 p.m., Calgary time. It was time to call Marcy and set up a time to meet.

"Hello?" Marcy answered the phone in a sweet low voice.

"Miss Murin, Sergeant Blair here. I arrived in Calgary a couple of hours ago."

"Welcome to *Stamped City* Sergeant, please call me Marcy. How are things going on the case?"

"Thanks Marcy. We've made some progress, but still have a ways to go." Rod diverted Marcy's question. "As you will remember, I said I wished to interview you. Can you spare some time tomorrow afternoon?"

"Sure, how about 3:30? Where do you want to meet? I see you're at the Delta, I can come over there."

"Fine, I'll arrange an office in their business section. I'll see you in the lobby at 3:30. Thank you Marcy." They ended the call.

Rod called Len, "Hi Len, I'm in town, can we meet at the Delta here in downtown."

"I'm about fifteen minutes away, what room are you in?"

"Room 1410, come here first, then we'll have dinner. "

"I'm on my way. I have some leads for you."

"I'm all ears." Rod laughed, as indeed, he was well endowed in the ear department.

What leads could Len have generated? He wondered as he waited .

Len arrived, gushing with information. "I'm into something good." He Announced, paraphrasing the Herman Hermit's hit song title.

"That good, is it? Don't sing it, just ell me about it." Rod kidded back to Len .

"I met a woman in Banff the other night. Her name is Shannon." Len grinned.

Rod teased him. "I figured you'd hone in on a woman! How does she figure into my case?"

"Inspiration! That's how." Len explained how he had uncovered the mysterious meeting between Cliff Murin and an unknown person at the Ranchmen's Club.

"How do you know he wasn't a stamp collector?" Rod handed Len a soda, and opened one for himself. Inwardly he was very interested in anyone Cliff Murin was associating with before and after Mrs. Murrin's death. He made a mental note to ask Marcy what she knew about her father's activities.

"I doubt that postage stamps were involved, considering it was shortly after the reward posting."

"You think there is a connection between the two? Yes, I can see what you mean! I'll meet with this Monahan guy and see if he can ID any of our suspects."

"Let's grab some dinner. I understand the steak dinners here are the talk of the town."

"Lead the way buddy."

CHAPTER 23

Rod languished in bed until nine a.m. He made some coffee from the fixings provided by the hotel and decided to contact Steve Monahan at the Club to meet him before noon. The old timer may have some more information to divulge.

Rod shaved and showered, donning fresh clothes he glanced in the full length mirror. *Looking better* he complimented his image. Organizing his files, he made a list of questions he would put to Monahan, with a separate list for Marcy. *He was curious how his meeting with Marcy would go? How would she react to the rather pointed questions he was going to be asking her about her father, Cliff?*

On a personal level, could he bridge the gap between work ethics and personal interests if she turned out to be as interesting and friendly as their phone conversations had been? Rod believed in mutual attraction principles, there was no scientific reason that explained how people react to one another, nor any way of predicting the outcome. The whole attraction thing could unravel like twine on a ball, Rod thought. He would let events play out, and then make an analysis of it at the end. Rod felt stimulated just imagining that there was some sparks in the old fire pit. His thoughts were interrupted when there was a soft knock on the door. It Announced the arrival of his room service breakfast he was famished.

The Ranchman's Club was still in its pre-lunch lull as Rod entered and Announced to the server that he was a guest of Steve Monahan. "He's already signed you in Sir, follow me to the dining room."

"Sergeant Blair, pleased to meet you." Monahan rose and extended his hand. "Have a seat. From our telephone conversation I understand you and Len Marks are acquaintances?"

"Yes, we use his profiling skills from time to time." Rod liked the straight forwardness of this old prairie dog. "We have been friends for several years now. Similar interests, you know."

"Sure, you wrestle criminals like we wrestle steers." Steve laughed, as he signaled for pint of Guinness to be brought over. "Now, let's get into this case of yours, I am intrigued in the fact that people I know and saw may be involved."

"You're referring to Cliff Murin?"

"Yes and his wife, Ruth. In fact, I knew Marcy and Lena somewhat as youngsters they were regulars at our Annual picnic. Once they turned sixteen I didn't see much of them here."

Rod took out a small notepad and began documenting the pertinent information Monahan was providing.

"I'm interested in the man you mentioned to Len. The one that met Cliff Murin after he posted a reward." Rod paused as he bent down and drew a file from his briefcase. "Would you care to look at these pictures, some may be two or three years prior to you seeing the fellow." Rod laid out mug shots and driver license pictures of Randy Romanov, Ken Ricci. Robert Sherwood, and a nameless Jamaican man in his mid-thirties.

Monahan carefully picked up each picture in turn and set two aside. "These two are not familiar to me at all." He had set aside Ken Ricci's and Robert Sherwood's pictures.

"Now, this one," he pointed down to Randy's photo. "He may have been the one. The man had a stubble beard of about a week's growth."

Rod, took a photocopy of Randy's picture from his case and sketched in a short beard, then slid it across the table for Monahan to view. "Does this make things clearer for you?"

"Yes, we are getting closer! Now mind you I can't say for certain, but that likeness would make me say I'm seventy-five percent certain. If I saw him in real life and saw him talking and making gestures I may be able to be even more certain."

"What do you mean by gestures? "

"I remember he drummed his fingers on the table top in a nervous manner, while he was talking to Cliff. It was quite distracting even from a distance of twenty feet, which is about the distance I was from them. Do you see that table way in the back and to the right of us? That was the table. And me, I was sitting right here, have been for twenty some years, since they remodeled the old building's dining room."

"Now, how about the photo of the Jamaican guy here? Why did you hold on to his mug shot?"

"That photo jogged my memory, in the third meeting between Cliff and your Clint Eastwood Guy, they were joined by a fellow of similar appearance. He was older maybe 45-ish and dressed like a very well heeled guy. He gave me the impression of either a successful business man or a high class sales type. I know that Cliff dealt with some big name companies in his property transactions. He may be able to fill you in on who the gentleman was. That was the last meeting I saw between Cliff and either of them."

"I will follow up on that. Now, tell me about your impressions of Mrs. Murin."

"Yes, most unfortunate. I knew her well, perhaps saw them in here five or six times a year. All the special days, like July 1st, Grey Cup parties, fund raisers, weddings and so on."

"Did you think they had a good marriage?"

"They seemed happy enough. Cliff was very successful, and she was a local celebrity because of her Olympic medals. Ruth was highly popular because of the time she spent teaching the younger swimmers."

"Nothing unusual then? Did you see them keeping company with other people?"

"Cliff is a pretty strong party guy. It's the nature of his business. But, I think he knew where the line was and he behaved himself. Since her death, I have not seen any real difference in his activities. He's working more hours. That's understandable, he has no one to go home to."

"What about his daughter, Marcy?"

"Oh, she's lived apart from them since she was sixteen. She was the wild one between the two girls. She's in banking now, settled down nicely. She went through a year or two of hell with a live-in boyfriend. I don't know how that got resolved but it's been over ten years now. She's a model citizen and a looker too, if you know what I mean?"

Rod, made a few notes and declined to speculate on Marcy's growing up experiences. "I'm glad we met. Your information may help us piece this all together. Do you mind if we stay in touch?"

"Certainly not," Monahan handed him a business card. It labeled him as a cattle trader. "I've been retired fifteen years, but still have several hundred cards," he explained as he saw Rod reading the card.

"Sounds good, thank you for your time and have a good day." Rod shook Monahan's hand, "and Sir would you keep confidential our talk here."

Monahan nodded, "Sure, I understand Sergeant. No problem there."

CHAPTER 24

Rod took a cab to the Calgary Police office to meet with Sergeant Mike Jones to discuss the Ruth Murin case.

He kept asking himself an obvious question. *Why would Cliff Murin be meeting with Randy? Randy and Cliff were on opposite ends of the tug of war over Lena. Why all of a sudden did they share lunch and talk business?* That was very puzzling indeed!

"Good to see you, Sergeant Blair." Mike Jones, ushered Rod into an interview room. "How is the crime solver of the West Coast?"

"Barely functioning," Rod replied as he eased his stiffening torso into a chair.

"Vancouver is a rough area. You should come and join us. Golfing and Skiing are our most serious activities." He grinned at Rod.

"I don't buy that Sergeant!" Rod bantered back. "Criminals and criminal activity never ceases. If you had a town of ten people there would be problems." Rod opened his file. "I have some information that may tie these two cases together or at least give you a reason to revisit the Murin drowning case." Rod described his meeting with Steve Monahan.

"I'll certainly review the file and keep in touch with you as things develop. I retrieved the file from storage. You are welcome to review it. If you need copies of anything give me a shout." Replied Mike.

"Thanks, I'll give it a once over. Check back in an hour." Rod settled back and began reading the reports in chronological order.

The initial report was dated June 28, 2008. The initial call was at 5:15 p.m. Cliff Murin arrived home to find his wife floating face down in the pool. Also floating in the pool was an upended Styrofoam supported floating chair. Mrs. Murrin's time of death was estimated to be 2 p.m. Initial indications pointed to a simple accident. She may have leaned too far over to one side, and the chair flipped over. The fact that she was an accomplished swimmer negated that type of accident. She had to be unconscious at the time of entering the water. The autopsy revealed she had water in her lungs so she was breathing while in the water.

The autopsy showed no sign of an aneurism or massive stroke or heart attack. There were signs of alcohol in her blood, along with chlorine and potassium. The pool was chlorinated and the medicine cabinet indicated Mrs. Murin was on multi-vitamins. There were no indications of bruising, choking or trauma.

Suicide was a definite possibility. It was ruled out due to the lack of supporting evidence and because of the strong dynamic personality of Mrs. Murin. She had everything to live for.

The coroner ruled the death accidental.

A check of Cliff Murrin's activities confirmed his attendance at a Real Estate seminar in Edmonton on the day of her death. He was the key speaker on the topic of *Sale of Businesses and Mergers*. His talk and lunch lasted until 1:30 p.m., then he drove the approximate three and a half hours back to Calgary. He arrived home just after 5 p.m. to find his wife's lifeless body floating in the pool.

A pretty tight alibi, if I must say so Rod said to himself as Sergeant Jones came in with two cups of coffee.

"How about a coffee break?"

"Perfect, I'm done here. Since this is your case I will leave you to question Cliff about that meeting at the Ranchmen's Club. I'll ask Randy in Vancouver and then we'll compare notes." Rod hesitated. "I have a suggestion. I'll get a tap on Randy's phone and see if he contacts Cliff after I ask him about that meeting. That may produce some new information on these two's activities." Rod closed the files and looked up at Mike with a smile. "Now tell me about policing opportunities here in Calgary."

"Be glad to." Mike reached in his drawer and took out two colorful recruiting pamphlets.

CHAPTER 25

R od reckoned he should freshen up to meet Marcy and went to his hotel room to change into an evening sports coat. He decided it would be best if he was prompt for their meeting in the lobby and headed down with 15 minutes to spare. He had seen a picture of Marcy in Lena's apartment, so he figured there would be no difficulty in recognizing Marcy.

Unlike Lena who had long dark hair, Marcy was as blonde as her sister was dark. It was evident by her strong gait that, like her mother, she was into sports and fitness. Not surprising, considering her mother had been an Olympic champion. She was beautiful and had a smile that went ear-to-ear. Rod began feeling a little bashful about his thoughts earlier on, but brought himself back to reality quickly and raised one hand with his palm open to shake her delicate hand. "Hi Sergeant," she said in a barely audible tone, not wanting to broadcast his status to the other lobby guests.

"Marcy, how are you?" Rod grinned but also spoke softly. "I'm so pleased to meet you." He turned serious. "Now come with me." He put his arm around Marcy's shoulder and guided her to the business office he had arranged. "I have a few questions to cover, which were too sensitive to ask you via the telephone. Please excuse me if I get too personal in some of my enquiries."

"Hey, anything that advances the case is okay with me. The sooner I know what's behind all these happenings, the better I'll feel, it's truly been so hard for me and Dad."

Rod opened his notepad and looked up. "Randy Romanov seems to be a part of the mix. You had mentioned that your dad and he were at odds about him dating Lena. Do you know of any other dealing between them, perhaps of a business nature, that would require them to meet?"

"I'm surprised to hear you suggest that." Marcy frowned and thought for a moment. "What period of time are you referring to? Randy has been away from Calgary for some time now."

"This was shortly after your father posted that reward money for information relating to your mother's death."

"Well, yes Randy was still around town then. However, if they met, dad kept that meeting secret from me. In fact, I asked him at the end of August if anyone had come forward and he said no. Perhaps he may have met Randy about some other business related matter."

"Any ideas about what that could be?" Rod looked up from his notes.

"Well, Randy was a union guy and dad had dealings in his merger department with unionized companies. Perhaps they had to reach an understanding as part of a business deal. Again, dad rarely discussed his work in anything but general terms. " She fell silent.

"That may be the answer." Rod looked up after making a notation. "Now, moving on to your family matters. How did your family get along during the last year that Lena was at home?"

"She was back east, getting her education. I was already out and living on my own." She looked away as she finished talking.

"I understand that you struck out on your own at a rather young age. Do you mind me asking if there was an underlying reason for that?"

Marcy was taken aback by the direct intrusion into her personal life. "I suppose it will come out. Dad was shall we say, *too friendly* with us girls. Mom finally caught on and arranged an apartment for me. She sent Lena back east to live with our grandmother. Lena finished school and university there, Lena was nineteen at the time. That made the situation tolerable for mom."

"She had to fight with her conscience as to whether she should inform the authorities about dad's deviant behavior. Dad insisted it was a result of the huge workload he always had to deal with. He kept reassuring mom he could keep his cravings under control."

RON ROSEWOOD

"It's a familiar pattern." Rod acknowledged. "That's a tough thing for young women to deal with. I'm sorry I had to dredge it up."

"That was ten years ago now, I can discuss it, even if I still don't understand it."

"It couldn't have been easy on you." Rod acknowledged.

"You're right, of course , it led to further relationship problems, but with some therapy I hope that's all past me now." The faraway look in Marcy's eyes conveyed another picture.

Rod responded, "Okay, we'll change direction here, how did you feel about your mom's death?"

"I agree with dad. I know it wasn't suicide, however it may have been an accident. Mom kept too much to herself, even though she put on a cheerful front, she was miserable and she drank excessively in the last couple of years."

"Do you think your dad's opinion of murder has any merit?"

"Not at all. It would be a stretch to come up with a reason for murdering mom. She was retired. She did community charities. She never upset anyone. No I think dad is wrong."

"Now, if your mother had no enemies, is there any reason why someone upset with your dad would try and get revenge by harming either your mom or even Lena , for that matter?"

"Hang on here Rod, do you think the cases may be connected? I never gave that any thought, certainly not about Lena. Dad is no angel, that business he's in attracts big money speculator types. However, like I mentioned, dad never discussed his dealings with us. Perhaps his boss could give you information about difficult clients. I know there was one lawsuit pending at that time that had to be settled."

"Did Lena discuss with you anything further about her decision about perhaps getting an abortion?"

"Yes, I was surprised that she didn't call me earlier. We had a short discussion. She was bothered by the fact that her boyfriend Ken didn't know she was pregnant."

Marcy continued. "She knew he was not responsible, but she

wanted their relationship to survive her being pregnant. She worried that if she told him about the pregnancy, their relationship would go south. I guess she was still working out some plan of action on how to deal with the situation. She never did tell me who her other lover was. This all goes back to dad's advances on us. It made us unable to handle relationships in a normal way." Marcy got Annoyed. "Damn that bastard dad of ours! Why couldn't he keep his filthy hands to himself?" Tears filled her eyes and she moved her hands to her face to wipe away the tears.

Rod was getting a clear picture of the family life in the Murin household. Things had not been anywhere near normal. Rod had sensed that when Monahan had mentioned Marcy having to move out at 16, that action usually suggests parental interference of some sort.

"Marcy, you've been put through the mill here, let's forget about any further questions, I can get back to you on anything further that I may need relating to the case." He checked his watch. How would you like to join me for an early dinner here? Then you can drive home in a more relaxed state."

"Thanks, Rod. That sounds great. I'd like that." She forced a smile to replace her troubled face.

"Great, I'll just run this briefcase up to my room. I'll meet you in the hotel dining room in about fifteen minutes."

"Perfect, I'll meet you there." Marcy spotted the restroom sign and hurried off across the lobby.

Rod wiped the sweat from his forehead as he entered the elevator. *What the hell am I dealing with here? I'll be an old man before this case is pieced together.* He reached his room and inserted his pass key in the slot. He stored his locked briefcase and noticed the message signal on his room's telephone flashing. "Who could that be?" He muttered to himself as he picked up the receiver and pushed the button to replay the message.

"I'm telling you one more time, Sergeant Rod, get the questions over with. We know where Penticton is! Maybe we should meet there, maybe at the funeral home. I hope we don't have to like do that." A chill overcame Rod. He recognized Steffi's voice.

"Damn that woman!", He hollered in frustration as he dialed Penticton. Plans for his family's safety had to be changed again.

"Hey Ann, listen you and Chris may as well take yourselves back to Burnaby the day after tomorrow. Take the flight that reaches Vancouver at 5 p.m. I'll be there to meet you. In the mean time, keep Chris and yourself confined to the house. We've had another threat. I'll alert the Penticton police to patrol your area."

"Rod, you're scaring me. Get this situation under control, I can't take this uncertainty for much longer."

"I know dear. We'll discuss it fully when I see you. Just do as I ask. The day after tomorrow at five." He repeated his instructions.

"Be careful Rod, we need you."

"Thanks Ann, we'll make it through this, don't worry."

CHAPTER 26

"Sorry, I'm a few minutes late, I had to make a call to B.C." Rod apologized as he joined Marcy at a dark quiet corner table in the dinning lounge.

"Hey, I took the liberty of ordering a carafe of wine."

"Great, you must have ESP, I could use a little mood-boost about now."

"What, a tall, tough Mountie needing a drink! Rod, you're shattering my image of the Force!" Marcy joked.

Rod laughed. "After all Mounties are human. We put our pants on the same as everyone else, one leg at a time."

Marcy laughed. "Tell me what your plans are when Lena's case is solved. Are you diving right into another one?"

"I have at least twenty open files, not all as serious as this one, but there is no shortage of work for us investigators."

"Like everywhere, I suspect. How do you sleep?" She hesitated, "No, forget that shop talk. Tell me Rod, do you ski?"

"I know how to put on skis and I know which way is downhill. Beyond that is sheer luck. My young lad leaves me quivering at the top of the run while he streaks down the slopes."

"I'm sure you're exaggerating Rod! Me, I'm what you would call an intermediate level skier. I suspect you must be at that level as well."

"I've got ten years on you, some muscles and joints are not as flexible and toned as yours."

"We'll have to arrange an outing the next time you're in town." Marcy noticed Rod grimacing as he shifted position on his chair, she remarked " I see you're stiff from an injury, was it job related?"

"I hope so!" Rod forced a grin. "I wasn't in any MMA matches recently." He laughed. "Let's order, I'm starving, what is your favorite?" He wanted to avoid any further mention of his gunshot wound.

"Let's see here." Marcy opened the menu. Seeing her favorite item was still on the menu she answered, "I'll go with the sockeye salmon fillet, and you Rod?"

"Let's make it two, I had steak last night." Rod got the server's attention and they placed their orders.

"Now let's have a toast to a quiet enjoyable stress-free evening." Marcy whispered as she raised her glass.

"My thoughts and desires exactly, Marcy. Now let me tell you about this ESP book that I am reading."

"Are you saying you can read my thoughts?" Marcy joked.

"Right down to your last thought. Now how do you feel?" Rod laughed.

Marcy grinned back. "Then I'm in trouble. I give up. Put the handcuffs on me right now."

"I think we can dispense with handcuffs. You don't look all that dangerous to me."

Marcy mimicked a serious face "Wait half an hour until this wine kicks in."

After dinner, Rod walked Marcy out to her car " Have a good evening Marcy." He saw her drive off.

Rod went up to his room to worry about his family in Penticton. Analyzing the facts, he was puzzled how his tormentors were so quick to locate him in Calgary. *Was someone actually following him? Was someone from the department leaking information on his travel plans? Was an airline employee involved?* Marcy had no obvious reason to stall the investigation of either Lena's murder or the death of their mother.

Monahan was more than cooperative. They didn't come any straighter than him. So Rod ruled him out. Sergeant Jones was a question mark. All Rod knew is what Jones told him. Jones stated he had been with the Calgary force some nine years and with the

RCMP for six years prior to that. Did he leave the Mounties voluntarily or was he nudged out? It would be difficult to determine the exact reason, from official records. Personnel files were closely monitored for confidentiality. Rod remembered that Jones had served in the Fraser Valley detachment at Chilliwack, B.C. Perhaps a little nosing around there would clarify details about Sergeant Jones.

Len Marks was an accomplished crime investigator and writer. If anyone had the credentials for committing the perfect crime, it would be Len. However, if the only motive was to do that, then Len would have to be paranoid. Was he challenged by his own work to put into practice his plots to prove that a person could indeed commit the perfect murder? *I must be going bonkers myself to even think that Len would be capable of murder!*

Rod made a few notes about his observations and decided to call Len and exchange information on the day's activities.

Len answered immediately. "Hi Rod, how did your day go?"

"Super! I met with Monahan and with the Calgary police . and then later with Marcy." Rod replied. Rod decided to soften his hand and see what Len might say.

"Anything new surface?" Len inquired in a soft, low voice.

"No, we covered the basic items we previously discussed. I have a few more things to follow up on. Just routine stuff. How about you?"

"I spent part of the day visiting my niece in an extended stay hospital. I learned she had a traumatic personal problem relating to her appearance in that junior beauty contest. I told you about that earlier."

"Was that the one where Lena won the main event?"

"Yes, the same."

"So, what happened to your niece?"

"She was assaulted by a man in the dressing room at the contest."

"Was the incident reported? Did she recognize the man?"

"No she kept it all to herself." There was a long pause, then Len added as an afterthought "She couldn't describe him."

"That's strange, did you know of this before now?"

"Not at all! Like I said, she kept it to herself until she had this breakdown two months ago. My sister informed me this morning, when I phoned and told her I was in town."

Rod did not want to divulge to Len that the likely suspect was Cliff Murin. Cliff could be dealt with separately when all the facts came out. Rod redirected the conversation. "When are you heading back to Vancouver Len?"

"I have a date with Shannon tonight, so I will be leaving for home perhaps tomorrow evening."

"Party time, is it?" Rod was familiar with Len's reputation with women from Len's younger years. Rod continued. "I'm leaving just after noon tomorrow. I need to get back to Vancouver before 4 o'clock." Rod did not elaborate on his reasons.

"I'll call you after the weekend then." Len offered. "It will take me a couple of days to drive back."

"Good enough then Len that will give me time to rethink this whole case. I have a dental appointment on Monday, so Tuesday would be a better time to call."

"Will do Rod, and Rod, have a good flight home."

They terminated the call. Rod now had some reason to suspect Len of being involved. He questioned whether Len was truthful in saying he did not know who attacked his niece. What better way to get revenge on Cliff Murin than to murder his wife and then a year later murder his daughter. Rod had a chilling thought, would Len, if he was indeed involved, go after Marcy next? Even if it was a remote possibility, it had to be considered.

Rod picked up his phone. Marcy should be at home by now. The phone rang and triggered the answering machine. Rod had no alternative but to leave a message. "Marcy, this is Rod, call me at the hotel as soon as you can. There may be a reason to take measures to protect your safety. Call me before you do anything else." Rod sat anxiously beside the phone. The quietness of the room accentuated his nervousness as the minutes went by, five minutes, ten minutes, and twenty minutes. Then the phone rang. "Marcy, is that you?"

"No Rod its Len here, why do you sound so panicky Rod, that's not like you."

Rod had to backtrack, he forced a weak chuckle "Oh it's nothing Len, Marcy left here after having some wine. I wanted to ensure she arrived home safely." He hesitated to see if Len had believed his explanation.

"I'm sure she'll be fine." Len assured him. "Now I'll be brief. The thought came to me that if Cliff did meet someone, it may have been to do with that lawsuit you mentioned. Quite often people meet without their lawyers to reach a compromise."

"That could be one of several reasons. But these people he met were not the lawyer type, according to the descriptions I have. I still have some work to do on that aspect of the case. I will see if I can re-interview Cliff when I get home." Rod saw the second phone line flashing. "I think I've got another call Len. Call me back in fifteen minutes if you wish."

"That won't be necessary Rod, we're done, and I'm on my way out, goodnight."

Rod switched lines. "Rod here."

"Hi Rod, what's this alert all about?" Marcy sounded confused.

"Marcy, I can only be general. If there is a connection between your mother's death and Lena's, then there is a possibility that you may be in danger."

"Why didn't you tell me earlier?"

"I was sidetracked by a threat against me and my family." That call came just before I met you for dinner.

"What are you suggesting Rod?"

"Do you have a girl friend nearby, who would put you up for a day or two?"

Marcy hesitated. "Yes, Claire, a friend from the bank has an extra room. I've stayed there on occasion."

"Okay. Arrange it. Go over there. Give me the phone number and address of her place before you leave."

"Yes, I can do that. Just a minute," she read the information to Rod, and added "Thanks Rod."

Rod cautioned her. "Marcy, call me at the first sign of anything unusual. I'll be here waiting."

CHAPTER 27

Back at his hotel, Len Marks, took a long look at himself in the mirror. He would be meeting Shannon in a few minutes. As he checked his grooming, he thought about how cool Rod had seemed to be. *Did Rod think that he, Len, was manipulating facts, and that he had some involvement in these cases*? "The hell with such silliness," he mumbled as he donned his dinner jacket and headed out the door. "I'm here for a good time and not to be suspected of being involved in a murder."

He strolled out the hotel doors and saw Shannon's car waiting. As he approached the power assisted door swung open. "Well! What service!" he exclaimed as he sank into the lush, black bucket seat. "You look sensational missy." He leaned over and kissed Shannon on the cheek.

Shannon grinned "Nothing but the best for the handsomest man in town."

"What fine dining place are we off to?" Len asked as she pulled out into traffic.

"It's only a few blocks from here, the Il Gogno Italian Restaurant, it's rated as Calgary's top dining place."

They arrived and entered the Il Gogno's brightly lit window dining room with tables covered in white linen table clothes accentuated by dark wine colored high backed chairs. The gleaming hardwood floor and the high pressed tin ceiling complimented the contemporary richness of the room.

"How do you like that Cowboy?" Shannon joked as they were escorted to their table.

"Spectacular, is all I can say!" Len pulled back Shannon's chair, then took his seat.

The server handed them menus. "The cocktail waitress will be right with you folks."

As they studied the menus, Shannon remarked, "It was lovely of you to call me."

"Did you doubt that I might not?"

"Well you know how guys at a ski resort are. Some of them are faster on their feet than they are on their skis."

"Perhaps the younger ones, at my age feet move slower and in a more direct manner."

The cocktail server approached the table. "I'm Marne, welcome to Il Gogno, would you care for a drink?"

Len nodded to Shannon. "You choose. I'm good with whatever you like."

"Do you have Rosso Della Valle 2007? I had that last month when I was here?"

"It's one of the most popular. A bottle to share?" she suggested

"That will be perfect Marne." Shannon smiled and turned back to Len as the server left "How long are you staying in town Len?"

"I'll be visiting my sister and her niece again late tomorrow morning. Then in the afternoon, I drive back to Vancouver.

"Then we had best start partying!" Shannon smiled as the wine was served. She nodded approval and raised her glass towards Len. "To you and I Len, and may the rest of the world wish they were here."

"That would make a crowded room!" Len smiled as they clicked glasses. "Well, I must say that is a good wine choice."

The evening was storybook. In addition to the luxurious relaxing atmosphere, their meals were superb. The desserts in Shannon's vernacular were "to die for".

While enjoying their meal, Shannon began exploring Len's likes and dislikes. The background music in the room prompted her to ask, "What is your favorite music and singer Len?"

"I like Ronnie Stewart, Elvis of course and the Beatles. Most songs from way, way back. I could never explain my tastes in music to my friends. How about you Shannon?"

Smiling, Shannon responded, "I like Stewart for sure, Tina Turner, and the new age singers like Diana Krall and Sarah MacLachlan. Real performers, I'm not into these new excessively synthesized musical recordings."

"We are getting old in our sixties," He remarked thinking of his parents with whom he shared many of their tastes in music. Len found it astounding to learn everything they were talking about flowed so easily and was interesting to them both. The bond between them grew as they continued exchanging experiences. They found it surprising how they could almost read each other's thoughts. Loneliness has a way of finding its way through mental mazes. Neither Len nor Shannon had ever experienced such an extraordinary feeling of closeness and kinship.

They took the server's suggestion, moving into to the lounge and dance area where the DJ was selecting his evening's music. Selecting a table and sitting beside one another, facing the dance floor and the DJ, Shannon whispered as she leaned against Len, "This is cozy!" She slid her body even more snuggly against Len. *Good* she thought. Len appeared to enjoy the closeness. In fact, she was sensing he was empowered by her forwardness.

The lights dimmed and the music started with a romantic ballad. Many couples rose to dance. "Shannon, would you join me in a dance?" Len said standing and offering his hand.

"You'd look pretty silly dancing by yourself Len," she laughed, reaching out to join him.

Never giving any thought to the fact this was their first dance. They began moving like dancers who had been together many times. Their bodies came closer to each other as they danced down the length of the dance floor. Len did not consider himself an accomplished dancer. With Shannon as his willing partner, he found he could move in response to her every step with smooth movements. The evening flew by as they continued sharing dance after dance. All too soon, the evening was ending. Their dinner party was over, however, the night was far from ended.

Driving back toward downtown, Shannon was trying to decide

how to communicate to Len that she was open to romantic suggestions. Deciding to fit it in to the conversation, she commented as she put her hand on his arm. "That was a delightful evening Len. I enjoyed every minute."

"You're a remarkable woman, Shannon. I'm sorry I couldn't stay a few more days." He said putting his left arm around her shoulder.

"Let's not talk about your leaving," she suggested. "Come up to the townhouse for a coffee? "She smiled, hoping he would accept.

"We had better ask your roommate." Len replied.

She saw her chance. "Actually, Cuddles my cat won't mind. She has her own room."

Len didn't hesitate. "Coffee it is then, my friend." Shannon leaned over and gave him a peck on the cheek. She had succeeded in encouraging him to take the next step in their relationship. She hoped everything would work out the way she had envisioned.

It was one a.m. as they parked in her condo parking area and took a slow leisurely walk over to her suite.

Shannon deliberately fumbled nervously with one hand and the key trying to open the door.

"Let me get that." Len reached out his hand grazing hers as he took the keys from her hand.

"Want to watch some TV while I freshen up?" She offered him the remote.

"Sure, let's see what's on." He began checking the channel display. He found the soft music channel and turned it on. Len wondered how things would unfold during the next few hours. He was experienced enough to recognize Shannon's motivation in inviting him to spend the night. That was his yearning as well. *Would his waning sexual abilities enable him to fulfill Shannon's expectations?*

Emerging out of the bathroom dressed in a light pink bathrobe, Shannon chirped. "It's your turn, lover boy." she smiled. "You'll find a man's bathrobe on the back of the bathroom door." Leaning forward she kissed him. Her bathrobe sagged open, revealing her bare breasts in the soft glow of the streetlights.

Len no longer had any doubts. "Too late for that sweetie," he remarked drawing her to him. Kissing her fully on the lips, he began showering her with short demanding kisses to her cheeks, her earlobes and the nape of her neck. Shannon responded returning each of his kisses, her nostrils flaring with excitement. She began breathing rapidly.

Their pent up passion was suddenly released and any thought of Len getting a bathrobe was forgotten. He was losing himself in Shannon's arms and charms. Feeling her smooth, velvety skin against his face, he started kissing her breasts. Feeling her nipples hardening, he responded. Gently lifting her, he carried her over to the turned down bed. In two swift motions, his shirt and trousers disappeared over the side of the bed. Drawing the sheets up over their bodies, they welcomed each other with their embraces.

With their desires met and their passions calming, they now knew they had more than minutes. They had hours to spend enjoying the pleasures of lovemaking. They were where they belonged. Every passing moment was strengthening their resolve. Destiny had brought them together.

After years of searching for contentment and happiness, Shannon and Len realized a solid relationship could develop between them. This was the start of a relationship that revolved around more than sexual attraction. It was the meeting of two spirits reaching in harmony for one another like high floating white clouds in a blue summer Okanagan sky.

CHAPTER 28

"Hi Marcy, sorry I'm calling so early on a Sunday morning. Would you have time this morning to meet with me, at say eleven this morning?"

Marcy hesitated only for a moment. "Is it about the case?"

"Yes, and I wish to explain to you as far as I can why I was concerned for you last night." Can you meet me here at my hotel. We can go for a morning walk in the area while we chat."

"I'll be there of course, I'll do anything to help." Marcy assured him.

Rod finished the call by suggesting, "We can have brunch later then I'll leave for the airport."

"Sure, I'll tell Claire I won't be back until later. By the way should I stay with her another day?"

"Yes, Marcy one more day would be advisable."

Rod was waiting for Marcy in the hotel lobby when she arrived. "Lovely morning, Rod" she exclaimed.

"Let's walk over to the park, it's only a few blocks from here." Rod suggested.

"Sounds good." Marcy agreed. Then asked, "What was all that fuss about last night? It kept me awake most of the night."

"I'm sorry Marcy. Perhaps it was my overworked imagination, seeing a villain behind every doorway" he blushed. "This morning you seem perfectly fine to me." Rod offered his arm. Marcy accepted. They walked in silence for a few minutes. Then Rod began leading into the reason for his wanting to meet. "Now hold on to your hat Marcy. I have reason to believe that your father may have been connected to an unreported case of molestation in 2007." He expected Marcy to pull away from him after his suggestion.

She tightened her arm against his. "That doesn't surprise me in the least. It was a dark family secret. That is why I left home at an early age. It is also why Lena was sent back east to school. We thought only our family knew, but I'm sure others close to us knew our family's dirty secrets."

"Why didn't your mother report the incidents?"

"That was hard for her, she didn't want the publicity. She blamed herself for being so involved with her swimming and not staying home to protect us. She did the next best thing. I got an apartment and Lena got shipped away. Now, Sergeant, tell me how that figures into your case?"

"The death of your mother and perhaps even the murder of your sister may have been revenge for his molestation acts against other minors."

"By whom, for God's sake give me a name!"

"It's only a strong hunch, Marcy. I have a lot of investigating to do. It may not even turn out be the motive. His name would in all probability be meaningless to you."

"So what's next?"

"I will re-interview your dad when I get back to Burnaby."

"He'll deny it all, like he always has." She began to shake and tear up.

"Words are one thing, but believe me, if I look in his eyes, I'll know." Rod reassured her.

"So what do I do?" Marcy murmured.

"Don't call him, or discuss this with anyone else. I'll call you on Tuesday, and give you a general idea of how things went. If your dad calls you, act ignorant of the whole matter. Don't even mention to him that I met with you or spoke to you about his molestations."

"That may be difficult to do. This is rekindling all those old horrible moments. I'm not so sure I can pretend that well."

"You're stronger than you think" Rod replied. They walked in silence for a few minutes then Rod saw Marcy begin to lose interest in the outing. "Now Marcy, let's turn around and go have that brunch."

Marcy clung to Rod's arm as they slowly made their way back along the tree lined boulevard. Nearing the hotel, Marcy had a suggestion. "May I drive you out to the airport Rod. I would like stay with you until you have to go."

"Yes, thanks that is a generous offer. I could use a bit of friendly conversation. cab drivers bore me."

"I'll try not to be boring." She smiled and placed her free arm across her body and squeezed Rod's arm with her right hand.

CHAPTER 29

Rod arrived in Vancouver in the late afternoon. Ann's flight from Penticton was scheduled for arrival at five so he decided to wait at the airport for their arrival. He strolled over to the coffee shop and sat next to the large windows that offered a panoramic view of the airplane take-offs and landings.

He envied the people that were flying out on vacations and other family outings. He promised himself he would treat his wife and son to a three week vacation later that summer. *Once this case is behind me!* He thought to himself. Surely, in three months he would have advanced to a point where he could turn matters over to the Crown prosecutor. *Who would the killer turn out to be? What would be the motive?*

A few minutes later, he saw the West Jet plane touchdown. Rod heaved a sigh of relief. They were here safe and he could protect his family. He returned to the carousel area and watched the passengers as they wandered through the gate. Then he saw them. Ann looked haggard and Chris still had his enthusiastic *I know everything* swagger. *It's good to be young and carefree.* Rod thought as they saw them moving his way. "Hi Ann," Rod hugged her. He turned to Chris, "Hi son how was that?"

Chris preempted a hug by extending his arm and shaking Rod's hand. "Better than school dad."

Within a few minutes, they were heading out the door. Rod noticed an enhanced police presence. He hailed a cab and within minutes, they were on their way to Ann's Burnaby apartment.

Ann had a suggestion. "Rod, can you stay the night at my place? I would feel more comfortable knowing we were together."

"That is a good idea, I was hoping you would ask. How about it Chris? Are you ready for some serious Poker?" The Texas Hold'em Poker tournaments on TV had turned Chris into a virtual addict of the sport.

"For real money Dad?" Chris fancied himself as an expert player.

"No, son, we play for bragging rights only." Rod admonished him.

"I want to be a millionaire by the time I'm twenty."

"I'd suggest getting a top notch education and working hard will get you there before lady luck does."

"How about luck dad?"

"Do you know what Stephen Leacock said about luck?"

"What did he say?"

"He said 'Luck is a funny thing, the harder I work, the more I have of it.'"

"You're witty dad!"

"No, Leacock is witty! Get one of his books, you'll enjoy the humor."

The cab, pulled up in the front of the apartment. "Thanks for the prompt service sir," Rod complimented the driver as he paid the fare.

"Have a good evening folks," the driver waved after he placed the luggage down on the sidewalk.

Rod looked around out of habit checking for anything unusual. He quickly ushered his family into the lobby and over to the elevator. Ann noticed his nervousness. "What aren't you telling me Rod?" she asked.

"I'll tell you in a moment," Rod replied nodding toward Chris.

"Mom, I'm hungry. What are we having for dinner?" demanded Chris, in a typical teenage tone.

"Dad and I will order some Pizza as soon as we have a short talk. Go see if there are any card games on TV. We'll call you when the pizza arrives."

"He's growing up fast." Rod laughed as he saw Chris close his bedroom door.

"He knows it all, like we did when we were young."

"Of course, we knew everything. The joys of youth ignorance, we learned and he'll learn. Now I'd better order that Pizza before he storms back out here looking for it." Rod found the number on the side of the fridge and placed the order.

He turned back to Ann. "Listen Ann, I'm not going to down play things. These threats are real and they're intensifying. I will stay here for a few nights until I can work out a better form of protection for you and Chris."

"How much longer do we have to worry about our safety Rod?" Ann remarked with a concerned look on her face.

"I can't honestly say Ann, other than to answer, as long as it lasts."

"That's a lousy answer."

"Hey, I would like the murderer to come to the door with his or her hands up and confess, however that is not likely to happen. In the morning, I will see if the fellows at the office have turned up anything since I left. I will keep doing my job, it all takes time."

"But it's all so personal! Why don't these people leave us alone?"

"They'll make a slip up, or have already made one. Time is on our side. Something will turn up. It's like looking for rocks on a beach, you have to look at a hundred before you find a keeper."

"I only hope Chris is not affected by this."

"He appears to be handling it fine Ann. Just keep tabs on his whereabouts."

"What about his school?"

"I'll take him there, every morning and pick him up afterwards. The only thing he has to do is stay inside and not go off with anyone. I'll talk to him in the morning when I drop him off at class."

The downstairs room buzzer blared. "That must be the Pizza. I'll go down and collect it." Rod rose to his feet. "Lock the door after me," he instructed as he left the apartment.

Stepping out of the elevator, he saw the Domino's man waiting at the door, holding two medium pizza boxes.

"I could have brought them up sir." He stated as he entered.

"I needed the exercise." Rod replied and continued "After we finish these pizzas we may well need some more." Rod reached in his pocket for his wallet. "How much do I owe you?"

"Twenty-two fifty."

Rod handed him twenty five dollars. "That's fine young fellow, thank you for the quick service." He accepted the pizzas, and turned away toward the elevator.

"Just a minute sir." Rod froze in his tracks and turned to turn to face the delivery boy, he expected to face a weapon. The delivery boy continued. "You gave me forty- five dollars." He handed a twenty back to Rod.

Rod smiled "So I did, I guess those new twenties stuck together. Thanks for catching that." Rod reached out with a sweaty palm and took the bill. "Good night, and thanks again."

Shit, is this case ever getting me rattled! Rod rubbed his sweaty palm against the side of his sweatshirt as he headed upstairs.

Ann opened the door to his knock and voice. "Rod, you're white, what happened."

"I took the stairs," Rod lied. "I guess I'm out of shape!" He handed her the pizzas. "I'll get Chris while you take these out to the kitchen. "Rod didn't want to add needless worry to Ann's already overflowing anxiety by recounting the downstairs mistaken incident. "Let's have a pizza party."

CHAPTER 30

After dropping Chris off at school, Rod headed to the office and called Corporal Smith into his office. "Has anything of significance surfaced on the Murin case?"

Corporal Smith opened his file. "We ran down some information on that Rex Trent fellow. It wasn't hard to do. He is sought after in the United States in connection with an possible investment fraud scam. Hundreds of people there have been duped out of several millions of dollars as a result of a Ponzi scheme. Meanwhile Mr. Trent has acquired during his short time here in Vancouver a four million dollar mansion, two light planes, and a yacht. He throws lavish parties for his many investors. He contributes, or rather, pledges huge sums to charitable organizations.

"Quite a mover and shaker is he?"

"I won't be surprised to see him disrobe someday and show a superman outfit under his clothes. The guy appears to be an absolute genius when it comes to promotion."

"Now, how can we connect him to any of this?"

"He has a Croatian born and raised wife, by the name of Stoja."

"Stoja? Could that be our Steffi? Now that is interesting! What else?"

"The firm where he got his start was none other than Devonshire Investments in Calgary. Recently the B.C. Government securities regulators tried to have Rex Trent's investor's license cancelled. His legal advisors got a proposed hearing cancelled by the courts, citing insufficient cause."

"He's well connected legally to be able to sway those regulators!"

Corporal Smith continued, "It appears the Devonshire Group is also trying to distance themselves from Trent's activities. According to rumors around town trust monies are not being credited to investors in the proper way. Several persons, contacting the Head Office, found there was no record of their investments on the parent Company's list of active investors. When I enquired at the Brokers' Licensing Division, they could not officially confirm that."

Rod replied "Could not or would not? They usually stay low profile, unless something goes public in a big way. We had better contact Rex Trent and get him in here. Do you have a number?"

"Yes sir, 874-2147 extension 1, as you would expect."

Rod jotted down the number. "Other than this Trent stuff, has any direct hard evidence been added to the Murin Case in addition to what we have so far?"

"We found nothing relating to the vehicle so far. The victim's cell phone is still missing. No eye witnesses have come forward."

"Could you call Cliff Murin and Randy Romanov in for this afternoon, say between two and four, get Cliff Murin in first."

"Yes sir and Mr. Trent as well?" Corporal Smith asked, as he turned to leave the room.

"Just hold off on him Corporal. I'll make that call." Rod winked at Smith. Rod had a plan that he thought might flush some pheasants out of the man's financial cornfield.

Rod prepared an authorization for a wiretap on the phone line of Rex Trent. He had a hunch that if this indeed was a larger conspiracy, a call to Mr. Trent might trigger a landside of leads. Rod hand delivered the request to Judge O'Brien at the Court House. The Judge raised his eyebrow when he read the name. "Rex Trent. I know of this guy. He carries a bright torch! This could get all of us in difficulty if it doesn't pan out," he warned. "Are you sure you want to proceed with this ?"

"We have reason to believe him or persons and firms connected with him have valuable information pertaining to our investigation." Without some new leads, we are heading for the *cold case* on the Murin investigation" Rod pleaded. "Status shouldn't be considered."

"Well, I too have a twenty-five year old daughter." Judge Duval said as he slowly reached for a pen. "Thread lightly, and let things develop." He advised, as he signed the authorization.

Rod felt rejuvenated, as he returned to his office and sent the order over to the telecommunication offices.

CHAPTER 31

Cliff Murin appeared with a puzzled look on his face as he approached Rod's desk. "Well!" he quizzed "Have you solved the case yet?"

"The leads are filtering in." Rod said as he looked down at his file. "I wish to get clarification on a few things from you, thanks for coming in."

"So long as you aren't suggesting Lena stabbed herself and then set herself on fire!" Cliff retorted sarcastically.

"Oh, I think we can rule that out Sir" Rod replied firmly. "Have a seat."

Cliff sat down without slouching. He looked alert and interested in what Rod had to ask him. "What did you wish to clarify Sergeant?"

"Do you frequent the Ranchmen's Club in Calgary?"

"Yes, a fine place. I go there perhaps three times a week. Sometimes with business clients, at other times I go alone."

"Now, I understand that you offered a fifty thousand dollar reward for information relating to the death of your wife. Did you get any response to that?"

"If I had, I would have forwarded the information to that lazy Sergeant Jones guy." Cliff's face turned red with anger as he uttered the name of the Calgary policeman."

"Shortly after your offer of the reward a witness maintains that he saw you with Randy Romanov, or someone resembling him, at the Ranchmen's Club. Can you remember such a meeting?"

"I'll tell you Sergeant, I wouldn't buy Randy a pint or give him the time of day! It must have been someone else in connection with a real estate or business listing." He paused. "What I can do is go through my appointment book for the weeks you are suggesting. My wife died August 29, 2009 I will cover from October 1 to December 1, 2009 and see if I can get a name for you. I probably had perhaps ten meetings over lunch during that period."

"I appreciate any names that may have a connection to the case. Now, around the same time you were seen with a well dressed Oriental-type fellow, do you recall who that may have been?"

"Yes, it was quite possibly Steven Lee Wong of Devonshire Investments. We were discussing the prospect of him financing some of the deals I was putting together. It was a general 'what if' type discussion. As you can imagine a sales contract only goes ahead if there is a source of financing available, we were setting the groundwork for that."

"Why would the CEO of such a large company personally come and meet with you? Surely they have other financiers available to promote their lending services?"

Cliff hesitated, "He never mentioned any direct reason. I suppose he wanted to stay involved at the grass roots level. You know, keep in touch with prospects such as me."

Cliff minimized Rod's hopes of obtaining anything substantive. "Getting back to my wife's case, keep in mind, Sergeant, other than a few crank calls from psychics, I had no serious calls and no meetings about my wife's death." He hesitated, then asked quickly. "Are you suggesting that there may be a link between Ruth's death and Lena's murder?"

"Until all the facts are in we aren't completely ruling that out." Rod looked at his notes. "Now I have another question for you, Mr. Murin. How often did you frequent the aquatic center where your wife instructed youngsters?"

"My wife died in our back yard pool Sergeant, not at the community pool. I took her a sandwich perhaps once a week. What is the connection?"

"We're looking for a motive, something that would involve you, your wife and quite possibly your daughters as well?"

Cliff was immediately silent. He gazed down at the office floor. "My wife and daughters were and are good people. No one was out to get them." He looked up with what appeared to be a defiant stare at Rod, as if daring him to say otherwise.

"You said at our earlier interview that you did not know your Daughter was pregnant."

"Well, I was just hoping to deflect your questioning away from what I consider a private family matter."

"There is no private matter when it involves a brutal murder Sir!"

"I understand that now Sergeant. I apologize for misleading you on that."

Rod locked eyes with him again and saw Cliff flinching and fidgeting. Silence again filled the room. "Mr. Murin, when are you returning to Calgary?"

"I have Lena's furniture and other things in storage. I'm planning to fly back to Calgary tonight." Cliff stood up. "Unless you require me to stay longer?!"

Rod rose and opened the office door. "Not at this time. I can call you if anything more is needed. Let me walk you out?" Cliff's gait quickened as they neared the exit of the detachment building. He had the appearance of a man that wanted out of there.

CHAPTER 32

Randy Romanov arrived at the office an hour later. He appeared somewhat less jovial then Rod recalled from their first meeting. "Sergeant how goes it?" he asked in dockworkers' terms.

"One painful step at a time, Mr. Romanov" Rod nodded to the chair. "Have a seat. I have a few more questions for you."

Randy sat on the edge of the seat, leaning forward with anticipation. "Fire away." He said.

"How familiar are you with the Ranchmen's Club in Calgary?" Rod said in a low deliberate tone.

"Yes, I've been there a time or two." Randy sat back providing some distance between him and Rod. He broke eye contact and moved his chair back a few more inches.

"Can you remember being at the club about two months after Mrs. Murin met with her accident?" Rod wanted Randy to know he had good reason for mentioning that date.

"I may have been." I can't recall the exact dates. I often had lunch there with people as I negotiated deals. It was part of my job."

"Did you ever have to negotiate any union contract business with Cliff Murin?"

"Not that I recall. No, there would be no reason to, he did not have unionized staff at his real estate and property investment business. He was not the owner anyhow. He was a commission salesman."

"Do you recall him making a public Announcement offering a reward for information relating to his wife's death?"

"Sure! The whole town knew that! It was in the news for two weeks running."

"Did you have occasion to speak with him about that or any-thing related to his wife's death?"

"What have your questions to do with Lena's murder?" Randy was getting aggravated

"We think there may be a connection between Mrs. Murrin's death, and that of Lena."

Randy shook his head. "I can't see that, two different cities, over a year apart! I just can't buy that! Where's the motive? Who would do that?"

"I have an eye witness that says you and Cliff had lunch and an animated discussion at the Ranchmen's Club."

"He's mistaken. That never happened. I told you Cliff had no time for me. He hated my guts. Believe me, the last person Cliff would have anything to do with would be me. Even the Devil ranks higher than me in Cliff's eyes!"

"Did you know Mrs. Ruth Murin?"

"Sure, she wasn't as hardnosed as Cliff. In fact she had a quiet charm about her when she wasn't doped up or drinking."

"What do you mean *doped up*?" Rod raised an eyebrow.

"On the few occasions I saw her, either she was on illegal drugs or on heavy meds.

"When was this?"

"About a year before she died, shortly before Lena dumped me."

"What do you know about Mr. Murrin's reputation around town?"

"He's a good salesman, a top producer every year, very successful."

"What about his social circles, did you see him around town?"

"I bumped into him a few times at a strip club us guys went to on Friday nights."

"What was the name of the club?" Rod began making notations in his file.

"Boom Boom's."

"What services does it provide for its' customers."

"It's a training club for young girls entering the business."

"You mean Nude Dancing, Stripping?"

"Yes, they look pretty child-like when they first start their routines. I don't think they get more then maybe half a day's instruction from one older stripper, Rena. Rena always closes the night by doing a more professional performance."

"Child-like acts? Can you give me an example?"

"They come out dressed like girls with their hair in pigtails, painted freckles on their faces and frilly short dresses. Most of the patrons were sneaky looking furtive types. They enjoyed these 'little girls' simulations."

"But you went also."

"Yes, for a laugh, we went to watch the other men spectators and even some underage boys that snuck in. Watching the crowd was more fun than observing the performers. I guess the word for it is slumping."

Rod added a few notes in his files and then stood up. "Thanks for coming in Mr. Romanov that will be all. I'll show you out."

Rod picked up the phone and called the telecommunications department. "Is the wiretap on Trent in place?"

"Yes Sergeant, we have it ready to record all calls."

"Good, I'm calling him right now." He dialed the number.

"Thank you for calling Devonshire Investments, how may I help you?"

"May I speak to Rex Trent please?"

"Sure, and who shall I say is calling?" A cooing female voice answered.

"Rod Blair." Rod said in a business like voice.

"One moment please." Rod waited thirty seconds.

A man's voice materialized. "Mr. Blair, good afternoon. Rex Trent here, how can I be of service?" His voice flowed like honey.

"I'm with the Burnaby RCMP, your name has surfaced in connection with a case I'm working on."

There was a long pause before Rex Trent spoke. "I'm well known. I'm not surprised that my name came up. I hand out perhaps five hundred business cards a month. That's a lot of people. Tell me, which case are you referring to?"

"Lena Murin, of the E.B.Taylor Mortgage Group."

'Oh yes, I heard of that poor girl being attacked. Doesn't do our image on the West Coast much good does it?" Trent began breathing heavily. " It's bad for investments out here."

Rod pressed on. "Did you know her?"

"Yes, I knew her in Calgary. Actually, I knew her father and mother better than her. More my age. However, I had some mortgage appraisal work done by her firm for us. I'd say we were acquainted, in a loose business sense, for about one year. Then, I was informed she left the firm. After that, we used other firms for our appraisals. I had no further contact with Miss Murin. In fact, I was not aware she was out here until I read the news report about her murder. A terrible thing." He fell silent, then continued. "That's all I know about your case Sergeant."

Rod determined he had said enough to worry Trent. "May I get back to you if the occasion arises?" Rod had added one more uncertainty to Trent's list of problems.

Trent reacted sternly. "Look! I'm a relatively busy man. I have a business to operate. If you wish to talk again, I would suggest you make an appointment through my secretary, and then we'll have a sit down discussion and go from there. Good day Sergeant."

Rod smiled as he placed the handset in place. *Sweet dreams Rex* he thought.

CHAPTER 33

Rex Trent sat back in his office chair swiveling his chair around and gazing at the ocean view afforded from his 26th story office. The blue pacific didn't seem as blue as it did a few minutes ago. He was worried. *What did this two-bit police mucker know that made him, Rex Trent, a target of a police murder investigation? Where was this Blair creep getting his information? What did he actually know? Was he shooting in the dark to scare up suspects?*

Rex was no angel. He knew his way around regulations. He could talk the feathers off a flying pigeon and be thanked by the pigeon when given back a few of the feathers. Nevertheless, this was different. Murder was a serious business. This was no white-collar deceit. Moving a decimal point here or there on a financial report to show returns was one thing, murder was something foreign to his type of business.

He looked around his opulent office and at his various framed university degrees, some real some merely for show. Numerous commendations hung on his walls. *I spent years getting here. Why should I take heat from a nobody cop? Who the hell does he think he's playing his Dick Tracy game with?*

Rex reached for the phone and dialed the Ontario number he knew well. It was the unlisted home number of Steven Lee Wong, the president of Devonshire International.

"Wong speaking" was the abrupt answer, followed by silence.

"Steve, Rex here. We need to talk." Rex paused.

"What about Rex, have the U.S. authorities extradited you yet?" Wong chuckled.

"Stop joking Steve, you fucking idiot. I can handle the U.S. agents. They are the least of our worries."

"Your worries , Rexie boy, yours, not ours. Leave me out of it."
Steven Wong warned.

"You shared in our dirty deals Steve. But forget that stuff. What I'm talking about here is murder!"

"Murder! What the hell are you referring to Rex?" Wong paused briefly "Start making sense Rex, or we're done here."

"Didn't you hear what happened to that *Lena* chick you were playing around with in the Bahamas for the last two years?"

"Lena, what about her?"

"She was stabbed to death a few weeks ago. I had a cop call me up here today sniffing around."

"What did you tell him?"Steven demanded.

"Very little, I had to admit I knew her and that we used her appraisal firm in Calgary. Then I told him Lena dropped out of sight in Calgary and we used someone else."

"So what are you worried about? You didn't do anything. I didn't do anything. So get off the phone and pull yourself together you God damn piece of crap!"

"Look Steve, if this grows, I can only keep your name out of it so long, sooner or later your involvement with Lena will surface."

"Let it! I'll deal with it then. You just clam the hell up and carry on with business as usual. We have a good thing going out there in Vancouver."

Rex suggested in a determined tone "Can't you get some favors from your political friends? Get them to turn the heat down on the securities stuff. Your Order of Canada should count for something."

"You have nothing to worry about! I told you, don't worry yourself into a jam-up. You can stall them with legal arguments for years, so relax. Let them investigate all they want. Now Rex, I have to go the kids want their bedtime story."

"I may have to call you again." Rex was not happy with Wong's *don't involve me stance.*

"I would say not. I'll be coming to Vancouver on Wednesday. I'll get word to you by messenger. Stay off the phone! Do you hear what I am saying? Just sit tight until we have our talk."

"Okay, let's leave it at that." Rex terminated the call. "Yellow bastard!" He muttered as he slammed down the handset. "If anyone had a motive to bump off that bitch Lena, it was him."

Rex began reviewing data on his computer and deleting anything that even remotely referred to Lena, or the firm of E.B. Taylor. Satisfied with his work, he drew the drapes on the fading sunset, threw some documents in his briefcase that he would store elsewhere and took the elevator down to the underground parkade. After looking around the parkade and seeing there were only a half dozen vehicles left in the parkade, he walked over to his to his Mercedes-Benz E-Class auto.

As Rex reached into his pocket for the keys a single muffled shot rank out, striking his pale and exposed neck. Rex collapsed to the cold concrete floor, blood gushing from his neck. The high impact expanding bullet had torn through his neck almost severing his head from his body. His briefcase flew out of his hand hurdling across the concrete, sliding and smashing into a wall five feet away. The briefcase lock sprung open tossing countless papers throughout the empty parking lot. A dark grey four door BMW SUV was a scant hundred feet away. It slowly pulled away and left the parkade while *Blame It on the Bossa Nova* blared from its stereo.

Blame it on the bossa nova with its magic spell Blame it on the bossa nova that he did so well

CHAPTER 34

Len had extended his stay in Calgary to be with Shannon. After all, it wasn't every day that an aging man could feel young and rejuvenated. He felt good, life was giving him a second chance for happiness. Now that he was back in Vancouver, he stopped his car at a florist shop on upper Kingsway and wired some 'thank you' flowers to Shannon.

Len had stopped to pick up Harry at the *Pleasant Valley Kitty Motel* on his way home from the airport. Harry was not pleased. The cat, didn't mind a night or two away from home, but a week! That called for payback, he began scratching and clawing at the upholstery in the back seat as Len drove. When Len arrived home, he decided to have a heart-to-heart with Rod, to clarify the matter of his niece's involvement with the Murin Family but just as he went to pick up the receiver, the phone rang, "Len Speaking."

"Hi Len, Rod here, listen I'm staying at Ann's place for a few days, do you have the number on your call display?"

"I'm writing it down as we speak. How are things otherwise?" Len was relieved to have Rod call him.

"Good, I think we are making headway." Rod replied in a guarded way." Did you turn up anything else in Calgary that may be of interest to me?"

Len chuckled, "Buddy the only thing happening in Calgary was strictly personal relaxation." Len paused then continued. "I'm glad you phoned Rod, I think we should discuss the Murin thing, so you don't have any doubts about me."

"Fair enough, let's do it in the morning, say 10ish, can you be at the office by then?"

"Perfect, I'll see you then. Have a good evening buddy." Len replied.

Rod came back to the kitchen where Ann was preparing to carve the roast of beef she had taken out of the oven. "Here dear, let me do that." Rod offered.

"Great, I'll put rest of the food out." Ann seemed to be enjoying the reunited family atmosphere that was forming. It was like old times.

Chris came bounding out of his room. "Are we playing Texas Hold'em again tonight Dad?"

"What about your homework?" Rod asked.

"All done, its math. I have no problems with math." Chris said proudly.

"Then Texas Hold'em it is! But only for an hour. Your mom and I have to discuss how we are going to handle the rest of the week."

"Thanks dad." Chris took his place at the table, and Ann served out the dinner.

The scene reminded Rod of a few years back when they were a happy functioning family. *Could those times be rekindled?* Rod wondered as he watched Ann and Chris interact. *How would Ann react to his suggesting a trial reconciliation? Perhaps, when the Murin case became solved and assuming no one got hurt, there would be an opportunity to bring up the subject. Yes, that would be the right time.* Rod would wait for things to calm down to normal, if there was such a thing in a policeman's life as normal. There would be a better time to broach the question of reuniting. Right now, he would enjoy a few days of togetherness.

CHAPTER 35

Rod couldn't believe what he was reading in the morning edition of the Province news paper. *High Roller Found Dead* he read the short report. The name Rex Trent jumped off the page. He had been talking to Trent less than sixteen hours ago. Now, Trent was dead. Rex's death must be related in some way to his case. He thought, it was too coincidental to have such a thing happen. Surely it has some bearing on at least a part of his investigation and his call to Trent.

"What's wrong dear?" Ann asked as she walked into the kitchen and saw Rod pouring over the article and strumming his fingers on the tabletop.

"Rex Trent, that prominent man about town was shot last evening." Rod said.

Ann wanted to know more. "Do you know him?"

"Not personally, but yes, I talked to him yesterday afternoon."

"And now he's dead!" She quickly drew conclusions from the facts Rod had given her." Rod, you're frightening me. Every day is spewing out what could be more trouble for us! Can't you put an end to this nightmare?"

"I can understand that Ann. Yes, this is a hell of an unnerving matter." He rose to his feet, walked over to Ann and put his hands on her shoulders. "Listen Ann, I am so sorry about all of this, you are strong enough to get through this." He lowered his arms and turned to pour more coffee. "I'm heading to work early. Keep Chris home today. I don't want either of you stepping outside for any reason."

Ann nodded, "I'll go tell Chris." She gave Rod a peck on the cheek, turned and left the room without any further comment.

Rod phoned Len and told him to cancel their 10 a.m. appointment. They agreed to meet the following evening at Monty's sports bar.

Rod contacted the Vancouver serious crime unit and discussed with Inspector Thurlow, the officer in charge of the investigation, his recent conversation with Rex Trent and his concerns with the safety of his family.

"Yes, that's interesting, let's meet later this afternoon. I'll come out to Burnaby say around three?" Thurlow was interested in what Rod knew.

Rod then called the technicians operating the wiretap. "What have you got fellows?"

"The guy has eclectic defenses against wire tapping, we totally got C-toned. But there was a call made to Ontario that lasted just over two minutes."

"Good, this indicates they are worried about who hears their conversations." "I'll do an end run around that. Keep the tap going they may slip up." Rod replied.

He requested the telephone logs of Rex Trent's business and home phone logs for the prior two months. They were on his desk within two hours. He began comparing them to the Ontario calls on Lena's log, there were twelve calls to two different numbers, matching those whit those on Trent's log he found both.

Both the numbers belonged to a S.L Wong. Rod checked his file and saw the name Steven Lee Wong was the CEO of Devonshire Investments. Rod could see why Trent was making calls to Wong. *Why would Lena be calling those numbers twice a week when she was no longer involved in business with Devonshire Investments? What was this interaction between Lena and Steven Wong? Could it be a personal relationship? Did it contribute directly to Lena's death?*

Rod looked back in his notes relating to the memos he had found on Lena's calendar . There was that ambiguous notation *Talk to him. Could 'him' refer to Steven Wong?* One of the phone calls coincided with the date of the memo in her calendar. *Did Lena have yet another suitor?* Rod remembered Ken mentioning that Lena had made frequent trips to the Bahamas while in the employ of Devonshire. *Were those more than just business? Had Lena and Steven Wong had an ongoing affair? Did the relationship continue even after Lena left Devonshire?*

Wong was a powerful man, influence peddling together with his millions was his forte. *Had all that prestige and influence won over Lena? After all, wealthy men crave Beauty Queen type companions. Was that the case here? Was Lena's promiscuity the direct result of the molestation efforts of her father? It all seemed to tie together. Did Lena have to prove to herself that she was still worthy of attracting a man's affections? Was this the classic manifestation of a sexually abused female?* Rod's thought process started to ask a whole new set of new questions in the case.

How could he tie Steven Lee Wong into the murder of Lena and perhaps Rex Trent as well? If Wong ordered a hit on Rex and had it carried out in the space of two hours, he had to have a well organized network of associates and thugs at his command. Who was the actual hit man? Rod scanned Steve Wong's phone logs but saw no numbers connecting any of the other people in his investigation circle. *Were the hits ordered in some other way? Perhaps an e-mail from a secret e-mail account?*

Rod continued to analyze. *With hits come payoffs, money has to change hands. What better way than to have offshore money paid into an offshore account that could be accessed in a year or two or three? Almost untraceable, as long as the funds are not moved around in large amounts.*

Rod continued to ponder. Wong had a motive for not wanting a child of his born and he had the wealth and connections to use offshore accounts. He presumably knew mobsters that owed him one. Rod knew he needed to question Steve Wong. He decided to discuss his hunches with his superior, Staff Sergeant Miller.

"Come In Rod. How are things progressing?" Rod entered and saw the morning paper on his superior's desk.

"Dead on the ground, like the headline on you paper there, Sir. However we have a strong lead now." Rod explained the possible connection of Rex Trent's murder to his case.

Miller listened intently. "You may be on to something. Now, the question is how do we penetrate the walls of this *Wong Fortress* and get a crack at the big man himself. "He is well connected sir, as far as big, well, I just happened to be in Ottawa when he was presented with his Order of Canada. He is six feet and weighs at least two-twenty-five! There is nothing diminutive about this Wong guy."

"That fits in with some other evidence I have." Rod described the size 11 shoes found in Lena's closet.

"Leave this with me, Rod. I'll make some discreet enquiries with my contacts in Toronto and Ottawa and see how we can go about isolating Wong and having a talk with him."

Rod returned to his office. Inspector Thurlow arrived a few minutes early.

He was beaming as he greeted Rod. "I have some video of the shooter leaving the crime scene." He opened his briefcase and withdrew a portable player. Together they watched the replay of the scene as Rex Trent began unlocking his vehicle and then crumpling to the concrete. In the background a dark colored SUV was slowly pulling away, it appeared the driver was talking on a cell phone. Again, the license plate numbers and letters were not distinguishable due to grime and mud. The tinted glass made it impossible to identify the driver.

"It fits the description of the vehicle my guy used in Burnaby," Rod acknowledged. Seeing the cell phone, he wondered if the cell phone might be Lena's. If it was there was a trace to the number he was calling. He made a note to check on that aspect of the case.

Staff Sergeant Miller's phone rang. It was encouraging news for Rod.

"Steven Wong will be at the Vancouver Trade and Convention center on Thursday at noon. Put your heads together with Thurlow and see how you can get a meeting with him. I'm sure he will agree to a short private meeting without any press involved. Send him a discreet message through his assistant. Use kid gloves as long as you can."

"What if he doesn't cooperate?"

"Then we go all out and nail him. Pin his Order of Canada to the Goddamn wall." Sentiment did not enter into Miller's crime solving equations.

Rod provided Thurlow with all the names and other details from his file. After an hour of back and forth theorization they agreed to exchange new information daily as they worked their respective cases.

CHAPTER 36

Rod leaned back in his chair, resting for a few minutes. Turning his thoughts to Ann and Chris, he was uneasy about the fact that they were still in an extremely vulnerable position. *If Wong's power was as extensive as it appeared to be, what could or should Rod do to counter the perceived threat that Wong might present?* He decided they needed to leave town. He called Ann and told her to pack for a two-week stay. Rod deliberately withheld the destination. He told Ann he would be there in a half hour.

On the way to Ann's apartment, he phoned his mechanic. In a few minutes he wheeled into his mechanic's shop and drove his car into a vacant bay. Gregor, the owner immediately closed the overhead door and handed Rod a set of keys to another vehicle. Rod took the keys and left through the rear door, sliding behind the wheel of a bronze GMC Jimmy. He parked at the rear of the building where Ann and Chris were waiting.

"Where are we going now, Dad?" Chris said with concern. "Where's your car?"

"Skiing to Whistler son." Rod replied tersely. "Never mind the car, get in."

"Why?"

Ann interrupted, " Chris, just listen to your dad, he's got work to do and can't be home every night." She blushed at her marginal explanation.

Resigning himself to the partial explanation, Chris climbed in, sat back and began playing his Texas Hold'em video game. "Can I at least go skiing while I'm up there?"

Rod nodded. "Ski your heart out! It should be great late spring skiing."

"Dad, are you staying?"

"Perhaps, when I come back to get you, I'll have a chance for a day or two of skiing." Rod accelerated over the Lion's gate bridge and headed north-west toward Whistler.

They arrived in the late evening and Rod checked them in under assumed names. They had a quiet family meal in the sparsely populated restaurant.

Rod arrived back at his townhouse at midnight to an awaiting message on his answering machine. A chilling message blared out. "Hey, Mr. Policeman, a bullet is waiting for you. Rex got his yesterday, yours is next. By the way how was your trip to Whistler?" It was a man's voice this time.

Chills crawled up Rod's spine and he took a step back and looked behind him. *Damn it, what am I dealing with here? Is this some sort of supernatural beings. They seem to know every move I make, even before I make it.* He realized that yet another character had entered the fray.

He immediately called the Whistler RCMP detachment and discussed his situation with the Sergeant in charge of the night shift.

"Don't worry! I'll alert the hotel security and I'll send one of my men over there for the night. At this time of the year, I'm sure we can arrange for him to stay in the adjoining room. Your family will be well protected."

Rod couldn't relax. He cursed the day he decided to become a police officer. *Why didn't I take business courses instead of criminology?* His mind raced through the sleepless hours as they slowly advanced toward dawn.

CHAPTER 37

Rod had another sleepless night. Before he left for work he called and checked on Chris and Ann and told them to lay low around Whistler village. Although Rod felt like he should head back up to Whistler, he knew he had to stay focused on this case. His and his family's life depended on it.

Rod reviewed Randy's arrest thoroughly and found that the more recent drug related incident provided no new information. As he dug down into the file, he came across an assault charge dating back to Randy's college days when Randy and Lena were living together. The victim was another university student. Randy and his brother, Maurice, had a bar fight with him over a minor matter that most likely was due to "liquid courage."

Maurice was four years older than Randy. *Was this the same Maurice connected to Lena's murder? If so, was Randy the person who ordered the hit or was he acting as a broker between the persons that made the hit order and his brother Maurice?*

Rod immediately checked Maurice Romanov's record. It followed a familiar pattern, the assault charge had been lowered to simply disturbing the peace. Maurice then spent two years in Iraq with the United Stated Military, where he was wounded and sent to Germany for treatment. Then two years later he was convicted of drug possession He spent nine months in jail. Apparently, Randy had gained some smarts since then. On the other hand, did he now work under the legal cover of Randy's occupation? Rod wondered if Randy was using Maurice as part of his persuasion team in his union negotiation work.

The thing that puzzled Rod was why would Randy involve himself in a hit that involved his former girl friend? Money or blackmail had to be the answer. Perhaps Maurice was approached directly by someone else.

A photo of Maurice projected a slightly older version of Randy, which certainly lacked any sort of charm. *Was Maurice the person that Monahan had seen with Cliff Murin? Was that meeting related to the death of Ruth Murin?* Rod figured that Monahan could easily have mistaken Maurice for Randy. He knew neither of them personally and there was a strong family resemblance between the brothers. That would make positive identification of either one confusing.

Rod was perplexed; this was certainly a new turn in the case. *Why would Maurice be meeting with Cliff? Did he murder Mrs. Murin and then put the squeeze on Cliff for more money? Was Cliff's scheme to offer a reward for information on his wife's death a way of diverting attention from himself and provide him with a conduit for paying out $60,000 not for information, but for the actual murder of his wife?*

The key here was finding and questioning Maurice. Rod prepared an A.P.B. on Maurice Romanov and registered it in the police computer system. He then dialed Randy on the phone. A sleepy voice answered, "Ya, Randy here."

"Randy, this is Sergeant Blair, I need you to come in and clear up a few more things on the Murin case."

"I'm in Las Vegas, Sergeant. I'll be happy to meet with you in a couple of days." Randy replied.

"I see, may I ask how long have you been down there?"

"I've been here two days now. I'm staying at the Aladdin. And no I haven't made any money yet." He chuckled then continued. "I'll be home tomorrow night and can come in around eleven on the following day. I'll call only if there is some delay."

"That will have to do, we'll see you then." Rod ended the call, thinking to himself, *very coincidental of him to be out of town the very day Rex Trent was killed.*

Rod ran a check through the B.C. Motor Vehicle license for Maurice Romanov and nothing came up. However, he did find an Alberta license issued to Maurice in February 2008. That indicated that Maurice could well have been in Alberta on the day Ruth Murin died.

Rod sat back and went over the new developments. *Who could tie some of these people together? Cliff? No, he was too involved and would not be forthcoming. Marcy? She may just have some recollection if a question about Maurice was put to her.* It was 9 a.m. Rod dialed Marcy's number. The phone rang twice.

"Hello."

"Sergeant Blair here Marcy, pardon me for disturbing you, have you a minute?"

"For you Sergeant I have all the time you need. Actually I'm off work today, I have a medical appointment later." Marcy replied..

"I understand Randy has a brother named Maurice. Had you met him or heard of him?"

"Yea, maybe. Now let me think. Yes, just after Randy and Lena split, I saw Randy with two guys in a bar at the Calgary airport. I was catching a plane to the Bahamas. One guy looked like he was related to Randy, in looks I mean. I did not approach them because of the strained relationship between him and Lena. I left the area before Randy saw me."

"What did the second guy look like?"

"He was a tall well dressed sort of oriental looking. I remember thinking to myself how odd, him being so tall. Usually the Orientals we see are barely over five feet tall."

"How old would you say he was, this oriental man?"

"Gee, maybe early forties? Actually, he was on the same plane as I, to the Bahamas. Does that help you?"

"It might be very helpful. Thank you Marcy, that's all I need for now."

"Call me anytime Sergeant, good morning."

Another possible link had been made between Steven Wong and the Romanov brothers, if indeed that was Wong in the airport. Rod was anticipating a lively discussion with Randy Romanov.

Two days later, Randy appeared somewhat unkempt as Rod met him at the front desk, "My flight was delayed. I just got in an hour ago." Randy explained.

"This won't take long, Mr. Romanov come in and have a seat." Rod led the way to his office. He left his file closed, but reached for a notepad. "I'll get right to the point. We'd like to talk to your brother Maurice. Do you know where we can find him?"

"Maurice?" Randy looked surprised. "He moves around a lot, Sergeant. The last time I heard from him, he was in Edmonton."

"When was that? Do you have an address or phone number?"

"That was about two months ago. No, I don't have an address or number. He lives with some German woman. He met her in the Military Hospital near Ramstein."

Rod made a note. "Do you have her full name?"

"I've never met her. Maurice refers to her as Mama. I gathered she's about ten years older than him."

"Ah. Do you know a man by the name of Rex Trent of Devonshire Investments?"

"Do I look like an investor Sergeant? Yes, I have heard of Trent, who hasn't? Why would you ask me about him?"

"He was gunned down while you were in Vegas?"

Randy again appeared taken aback "No shit! I guess he wasn't big enough news to score any press in Vegas, not that I read their news crap when I'm down there."

"I ask you again, did you know him or Steven Lee Wong, the CEO of the Company in Calgary and Toronto."

"Again, as I just said, I know of Wong too. However I never met either of them face-to-face."

"Someone saw you and your brother and another man who we think was Wong at the Calgary airport a few years ago."

"Hmmm, let me think. Yes, that was a while back now. I didn't realize that was Wong I think he introduced himself as Steve Lee. We just killed some time while waiting for a plane. He was off to the Bahamas. Maurice and I were going to Vegas."

"Do you know if Maurice ever had a meeting with Cliff Murin in Calgary?"

"Look Sergeant, my brother and I talk maybe twice a year. He calls me when he wants something, usually money. That's all. Except for gambling and girls, we have very little in common."

Rod saw he was not getting anything from Randy. He stood up

and said, "Thanks for coming in Mr. Romanov, call us if Maurice should contact you."

"Sure, I can do that, if I hear from him." He followed Rod back to the front desk.

Rod had one more thing to do. He looked up the address on Maurice's Alberta driver's license and cross-referenced it. Apartment 301 was listed as the residence of Steffi M. Meyer.

"Bingo!" Rod said to himself as he issued an A.B.P. for Steffi M. Meyer.

Shortly after, the phone rang. It was Staff Sergeant Thurlow. "I have a meeting with Wong at nine tomorrow morning, at the convention center. You are welcome to attend and to question him about the Rex Trent matter."

"I'll be there, let's hope we can pry some useful information from him."

"He's bringing his lawyer," Thurlow replied.

Rod was not surprised. "I would not have expected him to do anything different. I just want to look him in the eyes when I put my questions to him. He may lie with words, but eyes rarely lie."

Rod spent the remainder of the afternoon preparing for the questions he had for Wong.

It was lunchtime at the Zoo.

CHAPTER 38

Monty's Bar was moderately quiet on Wednesday night when Rod walked in and saw Len seated at their usual table. Motioning the server over and placing a drink order, Rod turned back to face Len. "Well Lennie boy, how did your Calgary stay go?"

"You wouldn't believe it, if I told you. Let's say it was a satisfying trip in all aspects except one." He continued in a serious manner, "I have the feeling that you suspect me of being involved in Ruth Murrin's death. Is that correct?"

"You did have a motive, considering your niece ended up in a trauma center because of Cliff's molestation. That triggered my thoughts."

"Agreed, no doubt about that. However, I would have gone directly after Cliff. Killing his wife was not a solution I would have considered. After all she was as much a victim of Cliff's as the girls having to live with the knowledge of his molestations."

"So you think it was an accident as the coroner ruled?" Rod hesitated as the server placed their drinks down and left.

Len replied, "I'd go 50-50 on that. There could have been other dads or uncles that would have reacted differently than I would." He reached in his jacket pocket and extracted a photocopy of a monthly planner. "It just so happens on August 9, 2009, the day Mrs. Murin died, I was in New York with my publisher, Dale West of the Bantam Dell Group. Here are all the contact numbers." He handed Rod the sheet.

Rod sheepishly accepted the page and stuffed it in his shirt pocket without any further scrutiny. "Okay Len, let's jump ahead here. I have some new leads in both cases, which may lead to arrests. So let's have a relaxing night out and see how things develop in the next few days."

Len nodded in agreement, beckoning the server for another round of drinks.

CHAPTER 39

Inspector Thurlow was anticipating Steven Lee Wong's arrival, as Rod entered the boardroom office that had been arranged for their meeting. "Come in Sergeant. Have a seat." Thurlow directed Rod to a chair beside him. "I'll start off the session. Then you can have at him with your questions relating to the Burnaby case."

"Thanks, Inspector, I'm confident we can make some headway today, if they agree to answer all our concerns."

"My presumption is that his lawyer will ensure that things are kept general. They will be out to learn what we know, while keeping from us anything of value to our case. I expect them, of course, to try and point us elsewhere." He was interrupted by a single knock on the boardroom door Announcing the arrival of Wong.

Wong was accompanied by his lawyer, who elected to introduce himself and his client. "Good day gentlemen, I'm Andrew Carter," he turned slightly and nodded, taking a hard look at Rod. "And this is my client Steven Lee Wong." He gave both officers his business card embossed printed with raised gold lettering.

"Come in gentleman, I'm Inspector Thurlow and this is Sergeant Rod Blair from the Burnaby detachment. Have seat gentlemen, we arranged coffee. Help yourselves, while I secure the door so we won't be bothered."

Returning to his seat, he began his questions. "Thank you for attending this meeting. As I mentioned in our brief phone conversation we wish to ask Mr. Wong about certain events that most definitely have or had some connection to his business interests," he paused and then continued, "And perhaps to his personal associations as well."

"We are here to assist in any way we can." Carter reassured the two officers.

"Firstly in the matter of Rex Trent, would Mr. Wong describe his recent dealings with Mr. Trent?"

Steven Wong didn't hesitate. He took a sip of his coffee as he glanced at some notes in his left hand. "Certainly Inspector, as CEO of Devonshire Investments, Mr. Trent worked for our firm in Calgary from January 1, 2005 until December 31, 2008." He stopped reading from his notes and began freelancing. "Rex was a provincially registered investment sales manager and he directed a group of thirty sales associates."

"He did very well and late in 2008, we reached an agreement wherein he would relocate to Vancouver and take over the office here. I felt he would be able to generate new business. The office here is more than a controlled branch, they have almost complete autonomy over operations. They have only to make monthly reports to the head office, and of course comply with yearend audit requirements."

"Is it accurate to say you were not in daily contact with Mr. Trent?"

"Our office had dealings amongst its money managers and other staff, so that would certainly be daily, however if you are asking how often Mr. Trent and I personally discussed business, my estimate on that would be perhaps once a week and perhaps not even that, if one of us was away on a business trip."

"Did you talk to him on the day he was murdered?" Inspector Thurlow asked.

"Yes, I received a call from him at home, it was at approximately seven o'clock Eastern time, four o'clock here, and he sounded rather upset."

"About what?" Thurlow interrupted.

"Two things. He was worried about the fact that U.S. Securities officials wished to discuss some of his investment brochures and some claims he and his salesmen were making. He said he couldn't keep ignoring their requests much longer."

"What did you reply to that statement of his?"

"I told him to proceed with whatever course of legal defensive action he was advised to take by his lawyers. As I mentioned earlier, he had full authority over the Vancouver Branch operations, he could elect to handle the U.S. people however he saw fit."

"And the other matter?"

"He mentioned that Sergeant Blair called him enquiring about his connection with the murdered woman, Lena Murin."

"And why would he bother to mention that to you?"

"I suppose because she had been an employee of ours at one time and we subsequently kept using her new company's appraisal services for some of our property investments. She was a very competent appraiser." Wong smiled slightly.

Thurlow prompted him to continue. "How did you respond to that?"

"I informed him that I had had no recent business dealing with Lena or her company, and if he hadn't any either, then he should stop fretting about it. I sensed the two issues at the same time took the fun out of his wheeling and dealing ways. Rex always liked being in charge. He always desired to be seen in a benevolent light. Appearing in control was good for his profile and therefore also good for business."

Rod realized absolutely nothing had been gained from the pleasantries thus far, he listened as Inspector Thurlow concluded his questioning.

"One final question from me Mr. Wong, do you not find it odd that just two hours after Rex Trent spoke with you regarding those two matters, he was gunned down in the parkade of his office building?" Inspector Thurlow let the question hang in the silence-filled room.

Mr. Carter elected to interject. "I don't see the connection. Mr. Wong took the call from Rex at his home. He helped his wife get the kids to bed shortly after that and they spent the remainder of the evening playing bridge with the neighbors from 8p.m. to 10 p.m. The insinuation that Mr. Wong was involved in criminal activities is a stretch gentlemen. I don't believe Mr. Trent's call to my client was in any way connected to his murder. Rex was Mr. Wong's most valuable operations manager. He had every confidence that Rex could mitigate his trouble with U.S. authorities. Mr. Wong assures me neither of them had any involvement in Miss Murrin's death."

Upon hearing the reference to the Murin case, Inspector Thurlow turned to Ron, "Sergeant, do you have any follow up questions pertaining to the Murin case?"

"Yes I have a few concerns." Rod looked directly at Steven Wong. "Mr. Wong how would you describe your business dealings with Miss Murin?" He quickly added, "I understand that she accompanied you to the Bahamas on several occasions in those early years when she was located in Calgary. She worked with you at times when you were in Calgary, as a staff member and later as an appraisal consultant. Did those trips involve any personal relationship issues? If so, how close were you two?"

Mr. Wong exchanged glances with his lawyer, who nodded to Mr. Wong to answer. "To be discreet about any aspect of our relationship, let's say we enjoyed the odd late night dinner on several occasions."

"And do you recall the last time you and Miss Murin either travelled together or enjoyed *an odd late night dinner?*"

"Let me think about that. Once she left Calgary, I did not see her very often. I had very few trips to Vancouver and if I did, my time was always occupied by extensive business meetings. However, I did see her late December 2009 at a Christmas party event Rex had at the Devonshire offices. It was on a Friday afternoon, it was about December 18 or 19."

"Did you at that time have personal relations with Lena at her apartment or elsewhere?"

"No, never! I flew home to Toronto later that evening."

"Now Mr. Wong did you at any time meet Randy Romanov, Maurice Romanov, or Steffi Meyer."

Steven Wong hesitated while he lit a cigarette, he seemed to be mulling over the three names. "No, not to my recollection, I do not know them, in any personal or business way."

"Do you remember a meeting with a couple of men in the Calgary airport holding lounge a few years ago?"

"That is too general a question for me to answer. As you can imagine, I make an effort to meet people everywhere and anywhere, that is my business, to be well known. If I met them, it was on a casual basis, like, 'look at the weather, where are you off to,' and that sort of thing. If it turns out they have investment funds available then I hand them a card or inform them where to find the nearest office of Devonshire."

"How about Cliff Murin, the real estate broker from Calgary?"

"Yes, I met Cliff once. We discussed business and property financing matters. His clients often needed money for mortgages, and lending is about fifty percent of our business. I authorized our Calgary office to do some business with Cliff's firm as a networking thing. I thought it could benefit both of our firms."

"Were you aware that his wife died in a swimming pool accident?"

"Yes, I was aware of it through my association with Lena. A terrible matter, that was."

Andrew Carter rose from his chair, "Gentlemen, Mr. Wong is scheduled to address a group of investors in fifteen minutes. I would suggest any more enquires should be arranged through me, you have my card. I have offices in Toronto as well." He shook hands with Thurlow and Rod, then he motioned Mr. Wong toward the door.

Rod showed them out and returned to the boardroom table, to review the findings with Thurlow. "That was a very clever duo, they told us almost exactly what they assumed we already knew!"

"Wong didn't become successful by being naïve! Was there anything new in what he told you?"

"He said he was never in Lena's apartment, if I can show he was then we might have some leverage on him. Judging from his feet, I'd say he was a size 11 ½ or so. " With that, he winked at Thurlow. Rod placed the Styrofoam coffee cup that Wong had used in an evidence bag." He had a smile on his face as he added a cigarette butt that Steven Wong had disposed off in the hallway sand tray.

CHAPTER 40

Rod was driving back to Burnaby when his cell phone buzzed. Slowing, he pulled over to the curb. It was the Whistler Inn, he assumed it was Ann calling.

"Hi honey," he answered. He was stopped, before he could say anything more.

"Sergeant Blair?" A male voice questioned.

"Yes, I'm Blair, who am I speaking with?"

"I'm Corporal English, Whistler detachment, I got your number from Ann Blair."

"Is everything okay?" Rod nervously enquired.

"Yes, she is upset, but unhurt."

"Upset! What happened? Is my son hurt?"

"Sergeant, your son Chris is missing."

"Chris! Missing? Can you elaborate on that Corporal?" Rod couldn't believe what he was being told.

"Apparently Chris and his mother were skiing on the intermediate slopes. Chris went down well ahead of Ann saying that since it was the last run of the day, he would see her back at the hotel. When Ann got down there about twenty minutes later and made her way to the hotel, Chris was nowhere to be seen. That was an hour ago. We have all the ski patrollers scouring the run and the neighboring areas. We have other men searching the village and the hotel. Nothing has surfaced yet." We need a photograph of your son as soon as possible."

"And Ann?"

"She is resting here in her room. I'm with her now. We're waiting for some news of Chris's whereabouts. I'll see if she can speak with you."

Ann took the phone, "I'm so sorry Rod." she sobbed, "I don't know what happened."

Rod was quick to stop her concern. "Look Ann, you did nothing wrong. We will find Chris and everything will be back to normal."

"Normal! Do you call hiding up here normal?" Ann collected her wits. "Rod when is this all going to end? I just can't cope with all this stress."

"I know Ann, believe me, I too want this to end. Let's just proceed on the basis that Chris is okay and we will find him safe. To do otherwise is not rational, other than he is missing, we have no information as to why, so let's just wait and hope for the best."

"Hope is a pretty thin thread Rod. I need more than that."

"Listen Ann, I am on my way, I'll be there in just over two hours. Ask the Corporal to call me at the first sign of anything, anything at all, which may help locate our son. Inform the Corporal that I have a photo of Chris and you on my mobile phone. I am sending it through to the hotel in the next couple of minutes, stay calm Ann, I'm on my way."

Starting his motor, and checking his fuel gauge, he pulled out into traffic. He made a couple of quick left turns taking him back toward and over to the upper levels highway to Whistler. He had no doubts about what was happening. Steven Lee Wong and his associates were tightening the screws even tighter. *What better occasion to choose than while the damn bastard and I are in the same room. Randy must have alerted him to the fact I was on to Maurice and his Steffi.*

How far would they go in their plan to hold Chris? Were they just doing this as a harsh reminder to Rod that his family was vulnerable? Alternatively, did they mean to inflict serious harm on Chris? In either case, Rod faced a dilemma, as a police officer, he had to remain impersonal. Though that was not how he felt at the present time. He was on the verge of seeking some answers using the old-fashioned Wild West tactics of one who shoots first and ask questions later. Now he understood firsthand how victimized and helpless people felt and how they reacted when facing a personal crisis.

Speeding northwest to join in the search, he kept observing

every vehicle that was coming his way. *Could Chris be in one of them? Was someone taking him down to the busy Vancouver area?* He scrutinized every vehicle he passed. He knew he was grasping at straws. The probability of him seeing anyone or anything was remote. He had a better chance of living to be 200. It was unlikely that a roadblock would be set up until the possibility of a skiing accident had been ruled out, or some eyewitness came forward with information that would justify roadblocks.

Rod worried about how Ann was coping with the stress of their missing boy. *Would she be able to deal with it? Was she going to relapse into the condition of a couple of years ago when she had to spend several months in a recovery home when her nerves cracked? This was no life for a family. Let someone else, perhaps more suited to police work and violent crime do the work!*

CHAPTER 41

Rod's cell phone rang, he put it on hands free so he could continue driving. It wasn't Ann's cell phone, the number came up at a private caller. He assumed it was someone from the Whistler RCMP search area.

Rod answered, "Sergeant Blair speaking, may I help you."

"How you doing Mr. Big Shot policeman. It is you that might need it, the help." Said the woman in broken English. Rod knew the voice was Steffi.

"What are you talking about? Who are you?" Rod feigned ignorance.

"Your boy, Chris, he is missing, yes?"

"What do you know about that?"

"We know everything!"

"What does your group want?"

"Come now papa, you know how to make it, how you say, make it the work."

"How? Make what work?" Rod waited.

"Like a favor for an old friend, I don't going to spell it out for a smart guy like you."

"Where is my son?"

"Very safe, yes safe, you can be happy, he's safe so far yet."

"Look, if it's threats we are trading here, I have one for you. It's called life in prison."

"If that is the happen, then you lose, we lose. We can do like you say, better, than that. I no want that, you no want that. Think about that like over the night. I call you about in the morning. You have the, as you say, the power, no?" The call ended.

Rod immediately called the Whistler RCMP, it was now correct to believe that Chris had been kidnapped. He was being held for ransom, not for money, but rather until the police investigation into the Murin and Trent murders wound down and ended up a cold cases. *That could take months, would these kidnappers risk holding Chris for more than a day or two.* Rod knew from experience that most kidnap victims don't survive seventy-two hours much less several weeks. Action, quick action had to be taken to resolve his son's abduction within that initial period. *How could he make that happen?* Rod was furious, he was certain his assumptions of the connection between Randy, Maurice, Rex Trent and Steven Lee Wong as the suspects, was quite likely correct. The sooner he could tie in some hard factual evidence and get them off the street, the better.

Rod called his office and instructed Corporal Smith. "Corporal, I need you to put a call in to the Edmonton police and get more information of the whereabouts of Maurice Romanov and Steffi Meyer and any other facts about them. Where they may have worked, travelled, lived, who their friends were and if necessary even the kind of restaurants or bars they hung out in. I think they are up to their armpits in these killings and we have to move fast in order to prevent any others. In addition, I also want everything removed from Lena Murrin's apartment and checked for possible DNA evidence. Tell the lab to pay particular attention to the ashtrays, cigarette butts, and condoms. I'll send the possible DNA match to the lab as soon as I arrive at the Whistler detachment."

"Sir, the rumor here in the detachment is that your son is missing?"

"Yes, Corporal, missing is all we know right now." Rod fudged. "I am within an hour of being there. Now just get to the task at hand and let me deal with matters up here."

"And I wish you every success sir, really I do."

"Thanks Corporal, I appreciate your thoughtfulness."

He went over the words that Steffi had uttered. *We know everything.* It was true how well they were informed, not only on Rod's family activities, but on the police investigation matters. *Did they have a pipeline into the Burnaby detachment itself?*

Then she used the phrase, *favor for an old friend* the very words Lena had been told. There was no doubt this was the same person. She was involved in Lena's murder, and possibly a witness in Rex Trent's shooting and now involved in Chris's kidnapping.

What could Rod say to her that might mitigate the danger to his son's life? Could he offer her money to buy Chris's release? Not likely! Could he offer her some sort of immunity or reduced sentence arrangement with the crown prosecutor? Not much of a possibility considering the seriousness of the crimes, and the fact she was controlled by more powerful people than herself. It was a dilemma.

Rod continued to play out the scenario in his head. There was of Ann's condition , she would be frantic once she became aware of Steffi's call. Rod decided he would shield her from that information until the time that it could no longer be kept from her. Sleep would be hard enough for her to come by tonight.

CHAPTER 42

Rod arrived in Whistler and went up to Ann's room. Knocking gently he heard her call out as she was approaching the door. "Rod, is that you?"

"Yes it is, open up." Rod replied softly.

The door opened. Ann ushered him in and closing the door and locking it with the dead bolt. "What have you heard Rod?" Ann looked at him intensely.

"I'm just on my way to the detachment unit Ann. I'll see what they have turned up." Rod looked away. Ann noticed his uneasiness.

"Rod, you are not telling me everything. Now stop lying, tell me what you are withholding from me."

"Ann, just let me handle it! For God's sake, you're in no condition to deal with this."

"No, I'm coming with you, I want to know everything that has happened." She reached into the closet and took out her jacket slipped on her shoes.

"Alright Ann, someone connected with that Murin case has taken Chris as a bargaining tool." He continued, "They assured me that he is fine."

"Fine! He's kidnapped and he is fine! Do you believe that? Rod, how stupid are you?" Ann took a step forward and collapsed in his arms. Rod collected her. easing her gently unto the bed. Sitting her down and taking a seat beside her, he held her as she began sobbing. "My baby, I want my baby back."

"We will get him back Ann. Just let us work on it. I'll call you an ambulance. Just stay here on the bed." Rod went across the room to the small desk, dialed the front desk, and made the request.

"I'll stay with you until they come. They said it will be less than ten minutes." Rod went back holding Ann as she sobbed.

She began pounding on Rod's chest and shoulders, "This is all because of you and your bloody career, why couldn't you be a banker?"

"There is no use going over things that happened twenty years ago." Rod held her arms in a loose grip "Just calm down and sit still."

They sat there without any further words until the ambulance medics arrived. After sedating Ann, they placed her on a stretcher and wheeled her down to the waiting ambulance.

Rod closed and locked the hotel room door and proceeded to the search unit trailer. The men were coming in from the mountain trails having been summoned by cell phone calls to call off their search. They were gathering around the trailer and informing each other of Chris's kidnapping. Rod approached the unit supervisor and identified himself. "I'm Chris Blair's father, any word or other findings on his disappearance?"

"Nothing from the men in the field, the village search unit has just advised me of a possible sighting. We have the couple at the detachment where they are waiting to be interviewed. You may wish to attend there to talk to them."

"I'm gone, let them know I'll be there in a few minutes."

Rod was ushered into the interview room. Seated there were a couple in their mid-twenties. A young beagle was sitting on the man's lap. An auxiliary police volunteer sat at the desk. "Sergeant Blair?" She questioned. An open file containing Chris's photo and a missing person's report were on the desk in front of her. "I'm Constable Marion Brewer. I believe this couple may have seen you son." Glancing at her notepad she continued," Their names are Walter and Mary Stockton, tourists from Ontario." She rose from behind the desk and stepped away , motioning Rod to come forward. "I'll let you take over the interview."

"Thanks Constable." Rod continued. "Now folks, start from the beginning, what did you witness."

Walter answered first. "We were arriving and proceeding across the hotel parking lot toward the hotel front door. We noticed a young lad with full ski equipment coming from the direction of the lifts. He appeared to be hurrying, almost running. In fact, his ski hat and goggles slipped off his head and fell to the pavement. He stopped to scoop them up in one swift motion and then he angled off toward the side exit of the hotel. He was about twenty feet from the building when a white van pulled up and stopped. That is when we lost sight of the lad. We heard a door open and a female voice call out 'We're from the RCMP Chris, your dad wants to see you.' There were some lower voices and I heard the lad asking where his dad was. Then a man's voice said, 'your dad is waiting at another hotel, he says it's not safe for him to come here, now, let's go." After that, I heard the clattering of the skis being loaded and the van door shutting. Then they drove off at a leisurely pace."

"Are you sure this is the person you saw?" Rod held up the photo of Chris.

"Oh yes, like I said his goggles and toque fell off so I had a clear view. I'd say ninety percent certain. He was dressed in a black ski suit with two white v 's on the arms, almost like a Corporal's stripes." Walter paused, his wife was nodding in agreement.

Rod, had no further doubts, he recognized the description of the distinctive ski suit. Rod had purchased it at Mt. Baker in Washington State only a few months ago. "Did they drive toward the highway or down into the village?"

"They drove down that road to the highway we had just come from.

"Did you see if they went east or west at the junction?"

"No, by then they were out of view on the other side of the hotel."

"How long after that were you approached by the searchers?"

"We checked in, went to our rooms, had a short rest, freshened up, and looked through some promotional brochures. That took about an hour and a half or so. Then we came down to do an afternoon walk around the Village. We were having a beer at one of the pubs in the village, when we were shown that photo of the Lad." Walter opened his hands and moved his arms sideways, signifying that was the end of his recollections and observations. "We thought it was a family matter of some sort."

"Did you get a look at the people in the van?"

"They were on the other side, all we heard were the voices. The only thing I saw was the driver's shoulder and back as he came around and got back in the van. He was white, below average height, stocky in stature. He had on sunglasses and a black toque."

"Did the van have any writing or company name on its side?"

"No, it was a cargo van, no windows on the side and had white wall tires. We rarely see those anymore, so I noticed that."

"How about the license plates, did you see any numbers or letters?"

No, I didn't think to look, I didn't even notice the color of the plates."

Rod could see he had been told everything these people knew. "That will be all for now. What room are you in folks, in case I have any other questions?"

"Room 1210. We won't be going out any more today." He looked at Mary.

Mary concurred "Not after something seeing something like that!" They stood up and left.

From the timeline of the couple's description, it was quite likely Steffi had phoned Rod about a half hour after they took Chris. That meant that he had passed them on his way up, if they had indeed continued through to Vancouver and beyond. The significance of the situation was not lost on Rod. He had the vehicle and occupant descriptions circulated on the police network. This was no longer threats or intimidations, these people were dead serious, Chris's life hinged on their mercy. Rod left the detachment and went down the street to the Health Unit to see Ann.

CHAPTER 43

R od approached the nurse's station and asked to see his wife. "She's heavily sedated. For a while we thought we would have to medevac her to Vancouver. I don't think she will be able to respond in any meaningful way."

"I just want to look in on her. Only a minute or two, I have to satisfy myself that she is resting."

"Come with me." The nurse led Rod down to a private room, shrouded in near darkness. Turning on a night light, she motioned Rod to have a seat beside Ann's bed. "I'll check back in a few minutes."

Ann was asleep and curled up on her side in a fetal position. Her breathing was labored. Her graying hair was disheveled. He noticed that she had scratches on her face. Looking at her right hand, which was resting on the outside of the covers, he noticed smears of blood. Ann had been clawing at her face and some of her blood had transferred to the bed linen.

"What have I done?" Rod whispered to himself as he held her hand in his. His mind thought back to the time she found out she had been pregnant with Chris. It had been such a joyous occasion, expecting their first child. They had upgraded from an apartment to a modest two bedroom bungalow. They worked in the evenings and on their days off preparing the nursery for the baby. Now fourteen years later, they were faced with their son's kidnapping, and Rod watching his son's distraught mother. As he stared at Ann tossing about, he vowed to set things right and re-establish some sanity to their lives. No one deserved to be subject to the threats and actions that he, Ann, and Chris were experiencing.

The nurse returned and motioned to Rod. "It is time to leave. Ann needs to rest."

Rod stood up and kissed Ann on the cheek. "When can I take her home or to a care facility near home?" He asked.

"Perhaps in the morning. A doctor drops by about eight. I'll get instructions from him then."

Without a word Rod nodded, and left the building. He did not want the nurse to see the tears forming in his eyes.

It was obvious that the kidnapping case had now relocated itself to the Vancouver area, and other than some tips relating to the van, there was little to be gained by staying in Whistler.

He would stay in the village for the night and perhaps take Ann back to Vancouver in the morning.

As he went back to the hotel, he mulled over the happenings so far. The vague description of the driver of the van led Rod to guess that it was Maurice and the woman was Steffi. He would work on that assumption until it proved otherwise.

Rod went over the events of the last several days. Rex Trent was been gunned down shortly after he finished talking with Steven Wong. Chris was kidnapped while Wong was being questioned by Rod. There was no doubt in Rod's mind that Wong was the kingpin in both these crimes. Wong was powerful, he had extensive connections in business, politics and in underworld circles. He would be a difficult suspect to build evidence against. The first thing Rod would have to do is convince one of the Wong Group to turn on him and make a deal with the Crown Prosecutor. If it was Steffi on the phone in the morning, she would be the first person Rod would try to persuade.

CHAPTER 44

After a fitful night, Rod was awakened at 6 a.m. by the ring tone of his cell phone. He knew who it was when he saw the *private caller* displayed. "Yes," he answered.

"That is the kind of words I like to hear." Steffi's voice seemed relaxed

"How is my son?" Rod barked back.

"He is, like you say A-1," Steffi laughed, enjoying Rod's discomfort.

"Let me talk to him." Trying to contain his anger, Rod calmly replied.

"Sure," Rod heard Steffi taking a few steps, "Hey sonny, your daddy wants to talk to you, now keep in the mind what I said about the thing you should not tell him, okay?" Rod listened intently for any background noise that would identify the location.

"Hi, dad." Chris's voice seemed normal.

Rod quickly replied, "Chris! Are you ok, did they hurt you?"

"Dad, I'm okay, I can't say any more." There was silence for a moment.

Steffi's voice replaced Chris'. "There is your proof papa, now you tell me what can you do for us? No, let me put in like, what can you do for you and your sonny boy?"

"Steffi, you have to understand that I am just a middle level policeman, I can't call off our investigation, if I don't do my job, someone else will get the file and keep working on it."

"You can like, do the like, pretend and run out of the leads, that's all, let it slowly go away, do your sonny the favor."

"Steffi let me give you another idea. You and Maurice can turn yourself in to the police. We will give you protection. You cooperate with us and you may get a reduced sentence for helping us."

"Protection, what protection did Lena have? What about big shot Rex? Your sonny here, is he protected? Do you know who you are talking about?" She paused.

Rod deciding not to mention Steven Wong's name answered "I know he's powerful Steffi, but only because others do his dirty work. If you don't cooperate either we will find you and send you to prison, that is the best you can hope for. Alternatively, he will get nervous and have you, Maurice, and perhaps even Randy end the same way as Rex and Lena? Believe me it will come down to that! Which is the better deal ours or his? You're a smart woman you can see that, ours is better, can't you?"

"You police are the same, tricking us, you have nothing. We have sonny here, what have you got?"

"The law protects you, you will go to prison, but you will be alive and can start over when you get out. Now, isn't that better than being found dead in a ditch with your throat cut and flies all over you?"

"Enough of this talking, now I will tell it to you like I did yesterday. Do not keep asking the questions on the case, make it go away. You will be a sorry papa if my people keep being like bothered by the police."

"Steffi, I will tell you right now, you and I will both lose, if you don't stop. Do you think the man behind this gives a rat's ass whether you or I for that matter, live or die? He will do whatever he thinks will keep him out of prison. You are just like a tool for him, once he knows you can't help him he will get rid of you. He uses people until he doesn't need them then they're gone, like last week's newspaper. Think about that and call me later." Rod hung up to reinforce the advice he give Steffi. When she didn't call back, he reasoned she was thinking about her options. Perhaps Steffi was the crack in Wong's armor that would completely blow the case open.

Rod showered, ordered breakfast and gathered up the entire luggage. He felt certain that he could take Ann back to the Vancouver area. He checked out of the hotel and left for the Health Unit building.

The nurse was expecting him. "I have good news for you Sergeant Blair, the doctor has cleared Mrs. Blair for discharge. He left a prescription for her. Other than that, she is almost ready to leave. I have a discharge paper here for her or you to sign. Stop by the desk on your way out."

Rod walked down the hall and knocked on the half open door. "Ann, it's me, I've come to take you home?"

"Come in Rod, I'm almost ready." She sounded calm. "Tell me, have you made any progress on finding Chris."

"Actually I talked to him for about half a minute this morning. I think perhaps something will happen in a day or two."

"What do they want? Is it money? You know we don't have much"

"It's just to pressure me into backing off on my investigations. I can't tell you any more than that."

"That's stupid. You haven't any real power to agree to anything like that. The police have to do their work. Where does that leave us?"

"Well maybe we can make them think we are cooperating. In the meantime we will try to get a line on where Chris is being held."

"Do you know who is behind all this?'

"I have it about eighty-five percent figured out?"

"Then why don't you start arresting people?" Ann replied as she flung the hospital gown in the corner laundry bin.

"We have to find some of the suspects. As far as the others are considered we need substantially more solid evidence."

"How long will that take?"

"Maybe a couple or three weeks, if we get a break."

"A couple of weeks! Rod, what about Chris?"

"I don't think they will risk hurting him. They know we can only offer them a deal if they look after him."

"I'm worried Rod, this is crazy! Will it blow up in our face? What if you quit the force? Wouldn't they let Chris go then?"

"I honestly can't say Ann."

"Can't or wouldn't? Give it some thought Rod. Which is more important your son or your stupid job?" Rod could see Ann was on the verge of hysteria.

"Ann, if my quitting the force would help, I would do it, instantly. I honestly can't see it helping. Now let's get you back home. We have to sign a release form on the way out. I have a prescription here that we will fill before we leave town."

CHAPTER 45

The drive back to Vancouver was a quiet one. With the aid of the tranquilizing prescription, Ann withdrew into a protective shell and spent most of the two hours looking at the Pacific Ocean with the passing of the freighters, ferries and other marine traffic.

Rod was concerned. He had seen Ann's withdrawn before. He knew it was just a matter of days before she might experience a mental collapse, prompted by pent up frustrations. He broached the subject of possibly getting her admitted to the hospital in Vancouver. "Ann, would you feel more comfortable in a hospital, rather than going home?"

Ann turned rudely gazing at him, "Rod, are you trying to lock me up again?"

"Don't be silly, I want what's best for you."

"Best for me? Get my son back! How about that?"

"Let's not go there! We're talking about whether you should go home. Chris's things will more than likely make you depressed."

"Depressed? You're understating how I feel. Depressed, I'm way beyond depressed."

Rod made a suggestion "Then you can see why you should consider a hospital stay for a few days?"

Ann resisted "No Rod! I have a better idea. Why don't I stay at your townhouse? That might be easier for me than going home."

Rod was pleased with her suggestion. "Sure, that's worth a try. We'll do that and see how you feel in the morning." Ann turned and resumed watching the sea traffic.

It was noon as they were nearing home. Rod saw a drive-in sign. "Ann, would you like some lunch?" Rod asked.

"Whatever" was Ann's terse reply, "I'm not very hungry, but go ahead. You have to eat."

Rod drove the remaining few blocks and parked in his designated space. They walked into the townhouse and Ann went into the kitchen, reached for the kettle and started running the water. "I am making some tea Rod" She plugged in the kettle and made her way down the hall to the bathroom. As she entered the bathroom, she saw a piece of paper on the floor. She bent down, picked it up and unfolded it as she straightened her body. "No!" She gasped. The note swirled down to the tile floor. Ann quickly turned and ran out the bathroom towards the front door. She fell into Rod, who was carrying luggage in each arm. Rod dropped the luggage and firmly held Ann's arms in an effort to keep her from crumbling to the ground.

"Ann? What's wrong? Why are you crying?" Pressing herself against him, she managed to utter four words between sobs "there's a note in the bathroom."

"Let's go back inside." Rod could sense this was more than imagined hysteria in her. He led Ann back in the house, "Sit here in the kitchen," he lowered her on to a chair, "I'll be right back."

Rod noticed the bathroom window was slightly opened, he assumed that the note had been easily slid through the opening. He grabbed the note and opened it up. In red writing he read the words, *this is your son's blood, his head is next!* Rod was overcome with rage, he held his breath as anger consumed his entire body. He felt the fury shoot out to his right arm and he punched the bathroom wall.

Rod quickly pulled it together. *I must stay calm for Ann.* He took the note into his den and placed it on the desk. Rod went back to the bathroom and searched for anything else that may have been left for him. He then checked the bedroom and the ensuite. Finding nothing else, he returned to Ann. "Ann, the bathroom is all clear now."

"I'm not going near it," she sobbed.

"Here, let me take you to the master bedroom. You can use the ensuite bathroom." He reached for her. Shielding her view of the main bathroom with his body, they slowly proceeded down the hall reaching the bedroom. "Call me when you're ready to come back out." He instructed her.

"I'm staying here. I'm not hungry." She went into the bathroom and shut the door. Rod sat and waited.

After ten long minutes Ann came out laying down on the bed and sobbing. "What are we going to do, Rod? We have to get Chris back before they hurt him some more."

Rod nodded "Don't worry, I think we are about to have a development in the case." He reassured her even though he was anything but confident. "I'm going to phone the detachment and get some security over here. Then I'll get Mrs. Sweeny, from next door, to stay with you. When I get to the detachment, I'll work out an action plan. Don't answer the door to anyone but me, and if the phone rings let Mrs. Sweeny answer."

"Do you want me to call her?"

"No wait here, I'll make the calls." He called Mrs. Sweeny, who obligingly said she would be over in twenty minutes to comfort Ann.

Rod phoned his office to ensure Staff Sergeant Miller would be available. He went back to check on Ann," here are your meds Ann, now get some rest while we wait for Mrs. Sweeny."

"How much longer will this nightmare last?" Ann moaned.

Rod tried to calm her. "We have them on the defensive. They'll slip up soon, that will be our chance to blow things wide open." He hoped he sounded more convincing than he felt.

CHAPTER 46

Rod arrived at the office and instructed the department's technicians to put a trace on his phone for last call that Steffi had made to him.

Arriving at his meeting with Sergeant Miller, he closed the door. He motioned Rod to take a seat. "Now Rod, we have a serious situation here with your boy, let's put our heads together and get things done here. We haven't much time to spare."

Rod detailed the sequence of events during the past three days and added. "We've got the technicians tracing that last call from the kidnappers. If they can identify the cell tower, then we will canvass the area for two things. First, we will look for the car rental agency in that area that may have sent out a white cargo van. Second, we'll try to locate the building in the area where they are holding Chris. They let me talk to him so they made the call from a room or unit where they are holding him."

"We've put additional men on the search for that Maurice guy. He's the most dangerous one next to Steffi."

Rod nodded. "If she calls again, I will try and work on that angle. Would it help matters if I convinced her that I was resigning from the Force?"

"Not in my opinion, she would guess it was just a ruse. She needs you on the inside hoping you will, at the very least, slow things down on the investigation." He put down his notepad and pen. "Now tell me, is anything happening on that Rex Trent case over in Vancouver?"

"I'll call Thurlow and see if he has anything new. It would be helpful if we could tie that case to my case. That will give Mr. Wong something to think about while he's jetting around the globe. He's well insulated so we have to work back up the line to him or whoever else is giving the hit orders."

Staff Sergeant Miller suggested. "I think it is safe to assume that Rex Trent was one link to Wong and his activities and it is what got him killed."

"If that is the case how do we get past Trent's involvement? If he didn't talk about it to anyone, and no one was privy to their conversations, then it ends right there. There would be no way to tie Wong into anything. You can bet any payments for hits are well disguised and made between off shore accounts and through an anonymous intermediary."

"Wong would have had to get some other hit group to take out Trent. Find that link and you may yet have a chance."

"Pray for me?" Rod smiled and waved his hand at Miller. "I have a better chance of becoming the next pope."

Staff Sergeant Miller stood up, signifying there was little else to discuss. "Don't give up hope. You may get something, you know a lead can appear from anywhere! Keep me abreast of your findings. Call me anytime, here or at home."

Rod left feeling somewhat more confident that they would see results, if they kept grinding away on the case. *One step at a time, Rod boy*, he thought as he went back to his office.

Corporal Smith beckoned to Rod from the bull pit area of the detachment. "Sir, we have a location on that cell tower, it is located near Grandview and Rupert."

"Good work, now take two officers and start canvassing the car rental companies and show them those pictures of Maurice and Randy, maybe we'll get a lead on the van. If that doesn't get results, expand the canvass to include the corridor West and North following the road to Whistler. They got that van from somewhere! I'll go and drive around in the area to find out what sort of buildings are situated there."

Rod knew from his general knowledge that the area was a mixture of commercial, old and new residential and industrial sections. His task in pinpointing the place where Chris was being held was going to be a monumental task. He would attempt to think like a kidnapper and see what materialized.

Armed with fifty photo copies of the suspects, he accessed the Grandview highway off the Freeway and spotted the 401 Motel. *Why not start enquiries there,* he thought as he worked his way around to the motel's entrance. The small lobby boasted a young male sitting at a desk reading his college textbook on economics. "Is the manager in?" Rod showed his badge.

"I'll ring him for you." The young man dialed a room. "Dad, a policeman wants to talk to you." Hanging up the phone, the student turned to Rod. "He'll be down in a few minutes sir, have a seat."

Rod began thumbing through a 2009 copy of reader's digest. He read a few notable quotes and other quick articles. A middle-aged man came pounding down the stairs. He had a quizzical look on his face "I'm Rashid, how may I help you?'

"We are canvassing the area looking for these men." Rod produced photos of Randy and Maurice. "They may have a woman with them that speaks with a German accent and they may also have a thirteen year old boy with them." He showed them to both Rashid and his son.

Rashid gazed intently at the photos, and then looked up at Rod. "None of our guests in the past few days resemble these two, and we only have six guests today."

"Here is my card, if they do check in. Be very careful and call me immediately."

Rashid placed the card near the phone and nodded "Sure, we will watch out for them."

Rod thanked them and left. He spotted a few restaurants around the hotel and dropped photos off at each location. At Rupert and Grandview, he spotted an area of old buildings that had once housed an Eaton's Warehouse Bargain Store. It appeared to have now been split up into several warehouse units. Rod drove around the building looking at each unit. Most appeared to be just that, a warehouse space only a few had actual offices displaying open signs. He drove around the building looking for a vehicle matching either the SUV or a white van, nothing!

Rod realized he had to think like the kidnappers. The places he was checking were places that would be avoided by them, because of the likelihood of being recognized. They would shop at supermarkets and shopping centers where they would meld into the crowd. As far as accommodations were concerned, Randy was the only one that had a permanent address. Steffi had only been in town less than a month from the indications Rod got from her conversations with Lena.

Maurice was from Edmonton, presumably brought in for the contract hits. Rod thought back to his interview with Randy. Randy had mentioned he lived relatively near the area Rod was canvassing. Looking through his file, he jotted down the address 1055 Rupert. *Would Randy be so brazen as to allow his suite to be used as a holding place for the kidnappers?*

It was a long shot, but Rod turned down Rupert. The house looked well maintained. There was a white Buick parked in the driveway. A concrete path along the side of the main house angled down some steps to a side door at the lower level of the property. Rod drove around to the back to see if there was back alley access. There was, however everything was quiet. There were no cars parked in the two spaces, obviously used by the tenants. There was a second suite entrance on the west side of the house as well with access only from the alley.

Rod drove back to the front of the property, walked up to the main house and rang the bell. A young Chinese woman answered, she was holding a six-month-old child. Rod faked a reason for his presence. "We had a report of a disturbance at this address. Is there anyone else here with you?"

"Only me, my husband is working. He's an auditor with the Canada Revenue Agency." She replied "you must have the wrong address."

"What about the side entrances? Do you rent out suites?"

"Yes, one is to a single guy, Randy, I haven't seen him or his car for several days."

"And the other suite, who lives there?"

"I had a German woman living there, she moved out yesterday."

Rod's attention heightened "Was anyone with her?"

"She lived alone. She was there less than one month. She gave me extra money because there was no notice. A man helped her move out yesterday"

"What sort of vehicle was he driving?"

"A white Van, quite long, she only had a few pieces of furniture and a bed."

"Did she say where she was moving to?"

"No, all she said was that she had to leave town for a job."

"Can you let me see the suite?"

"I'll give you the key, just a moment." She went back into the kitchen and returned handing Rod the key. "Lock it up when you leave and put the key through my mail slot. I have to take my baby to the clinic for his shots."

Rod hurried down to the back suite and opened the door. It was vacant except for a kitchen set and an old sofa in the living room. He took a few steps inside the suite and examined the few items of debris that were left behind. Initially, nothing of interest caught his attention. He went over to the kitchen counter and opened the cabinet doors where the garbage was usually kept. He pulled out a cardboard box to examine its contents. A few paper towels were at the top. Separating them, Rod saw signs of blood. *Could this have been blood from Chris, when they extracted some to write the message?* He bundled the papers up and stuffed them in an empty bread bag that was also in the box.

The only other thing of interest was a pocket book titled *The Wolf's Tale* by David Holland. Rod's heart skipped a beat. *Chris had taken it to Whistler in his backpack!*

Rod left the suite and returned the key to the main level. He would arrange a forensic team to examine the suite for prints and other evidence. He made a note of the property owner's telephone number that was displayed on the door for emergency purposes.

Phoning Corporal Smith, Rod had him put out an all points bulletin on the white cargo van with a notation that it may be on its way to Alberta. Rod had a feeling that Maurice and Steffi were returning to Alberta. *Was Chris still with them now that they were on the run? Would they regard Chris as no longer useful for their purposes? Would they let him live?* The alternative made Rod shudder. Those were his remaining thoughts as he drove hurriedly back to his office. His cell phone rang as he neared the detachment.

It was Corporal Smith, "Sir we've picked up Steffi and Maurice. The Kamloops RCMP are bringing them down. They will be here in about three hours."

"What about Chris?" Rod barked. "Sorry sir, no one was with them. They are going through the van as we speak."

"Did they question Steffi and Maurice?"

"They refused to talk, they asked for their lawyer." Smith replied.

"And who is he?"

"Let me see my notes say, it's an Arnie Silverman."

"Silverman! Ken, Lena's boyfriend used him when we first questioned him. Is that a coincidence or what? "

"Silverman is one of the best. He gets more than his share of business."

CHAPTER 47

Glancing at his watch for what must have been the thirtieth time, Rod was anxiously awaiting the arrival of the suspects. He had been advised by Staff Sergeant Miller that because Rod was involved personally with the disappearance of Chris, he wouldn't be doing the interrogation. Rod had apprised him of the items he had found at the suite that Steffi had occupied.

Arnie Silverman walked in and was directed to have a seat until his clients arrived. He saw Rod, but refrained from making anything other than brief eye contact. *Did he know that Rod's son was part of the investigation of his clients?*

Rod was anxious; however his only role in this was to monitor the questioning from an adjoining room and convey inconsistencies he heard while Maurice and Steffi were being questioned.

Rod sat at his desk staring at the case file when the phone rang. "Sorry Rod, but Ann is very distraught. She asked me to phone and ask if you have any news about Chris?"

"Mrs. Sweeny, I don't have anything positive yet." Rod fudged the truth. Hoping an encouraging report might come in about Chris. "Tell Ann, I will call her in about two hours. Better yet, just say I will be home early. Now, can you remain with her until I get there?"

"Yes not a problem." She replied emphatically.

"You're a doll, Mrs. Sweeny."

Maurice and Steffi arrived at the detachment and were booked on kidnapping charges. Arnie Silverman looked extremely unhappy after a twenty-minute private consultation with the two. "My clients may have some information you will find interesting." He offered as he entered the interrogation room with the pair in tow.

"We'll deal with that later, I'll ask my questions first." Miller informed them as he motioned them to take seats.

Miller addressed Maurice, "Where is Chris, the boy you took a couple of days ago in Whistler?"

"He is safe." Steffi interrupted "Randy has him."

"Okay then, tell us, where are Randy and the boy?"

Silverman answered. "They don't know, Randy did not say where he was going."

Ignoring Silverman, Miller looked at Maurice "Take a guess Maurice, you are Randy's brother, where do you think they are?"

"Randy, does his own thing, he told us to get out of town and he would take care of the boy."

"What do you think he meant by that?" Miller pressed the issue.

Silverman quickly answered the question, "They can't answer that, they don't know what plans Randy had. They have nothing further to say."

"Very well then, let's change the subject. What do you know about the Rex Trent shooting?"

"A terrible thing, that was. We heard it on the radio. We did not know him."

"How about Steven Lee Wong, do you know him?'

"No." Maurice was quick to answer.

"We have a witness that heard you on the cell phone with Steffi mentioning his name. Therefore, you can't say you don't know him."

"I don't know what your witness heard. He was wrong, I don't know a Mr. Wong." Maurice was starting to perspire.

"Where were you at 4 p.m. on the night Rex Trent was killed?"

"We were at the Hastings Park horse racing place." Steffi interjected." We lost a bunch of money."

"Do you know where Randy was that same night?"

"He was there too, he won the tri-actor in the third race." Maurice smiled.

Rod thought to himself, *how convenient! They were ensuring their alibis matched each other.*

Miller would have none of that. "Did anyone else you know see you there?"

Silverman looked at his clients they shook their heads negatively "There were five thousand people there," he replied, "Maybe the cashier or admission gate clerk will remember us."

Maurice quipped up," Randy paid for our dinner with a credit card, it was like about seventy dollars."

"Do you know what bank card he uses?"

"Bank of Montreal, for sure, he used that for years, even in Montreal"

Miller made a note of that, then he looked up "Whose idea was it to take Chris?"

Maurice and Steffi looked at one another and then at Silverman. Silverman spoke first "They have no answer for you."

"They got orders from somebody. Was it from Randy?"

"They have nothing further to say." Silverman stood up and motioned Maurice and Steffi to do likewise. He turned to them "I'll see you two at your arraignment tomorrow morning."

"What about the bail?" Steffi looked worried.

"Maybe tomorrow, you have to see a judge." Silverman stepped aside and allowed the custodians to take Maurice and Steffi to the detention area.

Miller gave him some parting advice. "Arnie, the sooner we get my boy back, the easier it will be for your clients."

"Look Sergeant, I'm with you. I've got two teenagers at home. I'm disgusted with this situation. However my duty is to provide them with legal counsel. Let's see if they remember anything more tomorrow. They might just have more to say. Maybe your kid will turn up by then."

Rod found Arnie's comments encouraging. *Was Arnie saying that Chris might be released unharmed, if the term unharmed actually applied. How could a youngster go through that and not be damaged both, physically and mentally?*

Rod thought about what he should tell Ann. Sure he had news, but it was no better than before. Chris was missing, and his entire safety rested with Randy, if indeed Randy even had him. Perhaps Maurice and Steffi were just saying that to shift the blame to Randy. There was a lot of rough mountainous territory between Vancouver and Kamloops. Rod's thoughts raced through his head. *It was very likely that Chris or his body had been left somewhere along that highway.*

Rod went into Miller's office. "That wasn't very productive, was it?"

"The only thing of value was the information about Randy's credit card, see if you can trace where he's using it. That may give us a lead as to where he is and if he indeed does have your lad."

Rod nodded, "I'll get started on that, if these two got as far as Kamloops then Randy could be well into Alberta by now. I have his cell phone number here, let me call him on the chance he is not involved like Maurice and Steffi claim." Rod dialed Randy's number.

He got the standard 'Hi, I'm Randy, I can't come to the phone right now, leave a message after the tone."

Rod replied "Mr. Romanov, this is Sergeant Blair, it is imperative that you call me immediately."

"I hate to say it Rod, but if these two are outright lying, where's the boy? Rod, we have to go public with Chris's disappearance, we may get a lead on his whereabouts."

Rod nodded "I understand and agree Sir" He turned to leave, tears welled up in his eyes," I have to take a few minutes to regain my composure."

Miller stood up reaching over and touching Rod's shoulder. "I'll tend to the missing person's report Rod." He walked to the door with Rod. "Let's hope for the best."

Going to his desk Rod drew up a production order to be served to the Bank of Montreal, pertaining to Randy Romanov's credit cards and other banking records.

It was time to leave the office and return home to inform Ann of the new developments.

CHAPTER 48

There was the smell of roast beef in the air as Rod entered his townhouse. Mrs. Sweeny had a cheerful smile on her face. "We've prepared your favorite dinner, Rod. Ann is resting in the bedroom. I'm somewhat worried about her. Except for a few minutes at lunch time she's been in there all day."

"Thanks Mrs. Sweeny, can you stay here until I have a word with her?"

"Sure, take all the time you need." She began setting the dinner table.

Rod knocked gently on the bedroom door and pushed it open. In the darkened room, he saw Ann half sitting half lying on the bed. He walked nearer "are you awake Ann?"

"Did you find Chris?" Ann turned on the bedside lamp and sat up.

"We found where he was held, and have two people in custody. We have a bulletin out asking the public to help us locate the third guy and Chris."

"Oh my God, they've killed him, they've killed Chris." She began weeping.

"Now, Ann, we don't know that!" Rod sat on the bed and comforted her. "We need to be patient and wait for the actual facts to come out."

"Rod, get real, you're a policeman! Do you honestly think that Chris will be found alive?"

Rod had to look away for a moment. "We can't give up, Ann until we know for sure, we have to be positive."

"Positive! We are up to our necks in your cockeyed case and you see that as positive? Well all I see is the beginning of the end, it's miles from being positive!"

"It's useless discussing this any further, Ann. I'll go thank Mrs. Sweeny. Would you like her to come in tomorrow?"

"Ask her to come in until noon. I can manage on my own in the afternoon."

Rod left the room and found Mrs. Sweeny in the kitchen.

She turned toward him "How is Ann doing? I just saw the report about Chris on the five o'clock news."

"She's very upset, we need you again tomorrow., at least until noon."

"I'll arrange things and be here at eight." Mrs. Sweeny gathered her shawl and purse, "I'll see you tomorrow then."

Rod decided to give Ann some time to gather her wits. He turned on the 5:30 p.m. news and viewed the report on Chris. The news report said he had been missing for two days and was believed to be in the company of an adult male in his mid thirties, a photo of Randy followed.

A few minutes after the news report aired, Rod's cell phone rang. The number on the display seemed familiar to Rod. He answered. "Rod Blair speaking."

"Sergeant, this is Randy, what the hell are you playing at, I haven't got the kid you're looking for. Pull that Goddamn bulletin off the air."

Rod took a deep breath, "Hang on Mr. Romanov, we have to go over this very carefully. Maurice and Steffi are in custody, we know they had my son. We know they were in the suite next to you. We know they had my son Chris in there with them Now they say that they turned the boy over to you. I tried to call you with this information, but your phone was taking messages. Now you tell me what you know?"

"Maurice and that piece of shit he calls his partner are lying Sergeant. I'm no damn angel, but I would not kidnap a kid. Yes they were next door, and yes, I lied about not knowing where Maurice was, put it down to family pride. I've been away in Prince

George the last two days, working with the pulp mill union up there. Phone George Hunter up there. He'll tell you the same thing. I just got back an hour ago."

"So you haven't talked to Maurice for two days and know nothing about my son?"

"I haven't talked to him since I got back from Vegas and saw you. He's nothing but trouble! You can have him and that bitch that's with him."

"Can you come into the detachment tomorrow morning and we can add your statement to the file?

"I'll be there first thing Sergeant. Now can you take my photo and that report off the air?"

"It may take some time Mr. Romanov. I'll see what I can do." Rod assured him.

Rod picked up the phone and rang and informed Staff Sergeant Miller, "We have a dilemma here. Rod, who is lying? Is it the duo or is it Randy himself? I would say we'd leave things as they are. As you told him, we'll look at it after he actually comes in tomorrow. Chris's disappearance is more important than some clown's feelings. Randy is involved in some of these goings on. He has only himself to point a finger at, would you not agree?"

"He knows more than he's telling Sir, I agree we will grind him down a bit further tomorrow and see what pops out of his mouth. Goodnight Sir."

Rod made up two dinner servings from the prepared food being kept warm in the oven. He took them into the bedroom. He was relieved that Ann had not turned on the bedroom TV. "I have a plate of dinner for you Ann. You have to eat. He placed the food on the night table and sat in a nearby side chair balancing his plate on his knees.

"I heard you on the phone Rod, has anything happened?" Ann enquired.

"Just checking with some of the people I have to see tomorrow morning."

"Has it anything to do with Chris?"

"Not directly Ann." Rod lied, he wanted to keep things as calm as possible.

"Turn on the TV would you," Ann directed.

"What channel?"

"35 the m8vie channel, let's see what's on there."

Rod thought *good she won't get the news report on there.* "Is that loud enough?"

"Yes." Ann picked at her food and took a few mouthfuls then handed the plate to Rod. "Here put this in the fridge I may have some later."

"I'll be in the den doing some paperwork. Call me if you need anything."

CHAPTER 49

Rod sat down at his desk in his den, picked up the phone and called Len to explain the developments of the past two days.

"I just saw the report and recognized Chris's face Rod. I'm sorry to hear this. How can I help?"

"What's your quick assessment?"

"It does not look promising, they had no further leverage with Chris and so he was dispensable. If they killed those two other people, it is more than likely they left Chris dead somewhere along the highway on their way up to Kamloops. I'm sorry to be so blunt Rod, but that is my prediction. I hope I am proved wrong."

"I agree, we have to start leaning that way Len. I'm really concerned about Ann. In a few hours she will know everything. She's teetering on the brink of psychosis at the moment. She can't handle any more bad news."

"Stay with her 24-7 or get her into a hospital situation right away. I remember the last time she had a meltdown. These things worsen each time. If she regresses, you may lose her completely."

"I have a neighbor lady coming in the morning. I'll instruct her to keep the TV and radio off."

"Would you like me to drop by and see her, I could give her a listening partner, it may help her."

"She would sense things have gotten worse, let's just see how the morning goes. I'll take your advice about a hospital if she's becomes worse."

"Okay then Rod, hang in there. I'll wait to hear from you. Phone me anytime. Goodnight."

Rod decided to spend some time with Ann. He left his den and walked toward the bedroom.

"I thought you had some work to do?" She said as he entered the room.

"It can wait. This is more important. What are you watching?"

"An old Jerry Lewis movie, he reminds me of Jim Carey."

Rod drew an analogy. "It's more a case of Jim Carey parroting Lewis' methods. If something is successful why not make use of it?"

"It's half way through."

"No matter, I'll watch it with you." Rod dragged the armchair over beside the bed to face the TV. He took a longingly gaze over at Ann as she watched the movie. He pondered his life, the good times and bad times and how unfair it was at this very moment. *What will this do to our relationship?* He only saw dark.

CHAPTER 50

The next morning shortly after arriving at work, Rod began reviewing his case files to refresh his memory.

Staff Sergeant Miller knocked lightly on the door jamb. Stepping into the room and closing the door, he spoke softly. "Sorry to interrupt you Rod," he walked over to Rod's desk but remained standing, "We just got a report in from Manning Park," He paused momentarily, "they found Chris's body."

Rod sat motionless in his chair. He did not want to believe what he had just heard. "Are you sure it was Chris?"

"Yes, we are sure. The description matches and there is no doubt as far as the Hope detachment is concerned. They have a copy of Chris's photo."

"How did he die?"

"It appears like suffocation, there were no other serious wounds on his body."

"Where did they find him?"

"On the road up to the Gibson Pass ski hill, an employee was installing a summer closure sign across the road about two miles from the top. He went over to the rest area to use the outhouse and found Chris' body a few feet from the path. The Hope detachment is doing forensic work up at the site. They're sending the body to Burnaby General Hospital for the autopsy. You can make a positive identification there. That's all we have right for now. I'm so sorry Rod." He reached down and put his hand on Rod's shoulder.

Rod nodded slowly standing up, then he slumped back down into his chair. "I have to go see Ann before she gets the news from someone else." He stood up and handed a file to Miller. "I've got

Randy Romanov coming in this morning. Would you deal with him? There's a sheet with my questions in the file."

Miller reached for the file. "Sure Rod, you go ahead, take as much time as you need. We have to get the truth out of these weasels one way or another." Miller turned and left.

Rod sat down again. He began mulling over how he would break the news to Ann. She would be devastated. *Could she handle the impact of hearing their only child was dead. What could he say? How would she react?*

Rod felt partly responsible. *Could he have forestalled this by easing off the investigation?* Surely he wasn't the first policeman that had a reason to slacken off a case. *Should he have made a decision to do things differently? Instead of being a body in the morgue, would Chris be a happy, enthusiastic, school boy?* Rod regretted not choosing another career path.

Miller could see Randy walking from his car to the office entrance. He went to the front desk and ushered him to the interview room. "Have a seat Mr. Romanov, we have a new development in the case." He continued "We found Chris's body this morning."

Randy turned pale "I'm sorry to hear that. Do you still wish to talk to me?"

"Oh yes. More than ever. By the end of tomorrow we will have enough evidence to charge all three of you with murder. You, your brother and the woman, Steffi."

"Come now, leave me out of it. I told Sergeant Blair, I was in Prince George!"

"Isn't it coincidental that you are always out of town when these people you are involved with are either committing a murder or are the victims."

"So what! It only proves I didn't do anything." Randy stayed standing.

"It's more than coincidence." Miller glanced at the notes and questions Rod had prepared. "When Lena was murdered you were at the income tax office. When Rex Trent was murdered you were in Vegas. Now when my Officer's son is murdered, you are on your way home from Prince George. That seems odd to us!"

"Odd or not, like I said, I'm not involved. I had nothing to do with it."

"Maurice said you were with him at the racetrack when Trent was killed? You say you were in Vegas? Now, which is it?"

"Maurice is lying!"

"He said you used your credit card at the track. We are getting details from the Bank of Montreal right now! How can you explain that?"

"I lent Maurice my card. He's always out of money. He said he was not able to cover his expenses. After all he is my brother."

"We found no card on him or Steffi when we booked them yesterday."

"He put the card through my mail slot. I found it when I returned from Prince George."

"Why would he give it back to you when he was facing costly travel bills?"

"That's him, just stupid as usual, he has to answer that! Maybe he got some money from elsewhere."

"Look Mr. Romanov, you are a very clever operator. You know more about these murders than you are divulging. Now, why don't you cooperate with us and stop misleading us?"

"Do I need a lawyer?"

" You have that option. Are you requesting a lawyer to be present?"

"Well no, go ahead ask some more questions. I'll decide when I need a lawyer. I did not kill anyone."

"What do you know about Lena Murin and Steven Wong?"

"She worked for him in Calgary."

"I mean about a personal affair?"

"I was out of the loop three months after she relocated to Calgary. I never heard of any affair."

"When she talked about her pregnancy, did she mention anything that gave you an idea who the man might be?"

"Because he wanted her to get an abortion, then I would assume he was a married man and an influential person, I watch dramas on TV all the time. It's the same pattern."

"That describes Wong, does it not?" Miller made some notes in his file.

Randy paled motioning to Miller with both arms outstretched , palms up. "Hey what are you writing down? I never said anything about Steven Wong."

"You'll agree he fits the type of person you described?"

"And every second rich playboy guy in Canada. Don't put words in my mouth."

"Do you regard Wong as a dangerous person?"

"I don't know him that well." Randy's demeanor said different, he appeared scared.

"What about Maurice and Steffi, do they work for him?"

"Maurice does his own thing. I don't know anything more about him or Wong or anyone else."

"I suggest that Maurice does in fact get work from you and you are a middleman with many of his persuasive assignments."

"Not in these cases. I have no more to say. I want a lawyer. May I go now?"

"I need to consult with the Chief of the detachment. Wait here a minute."

Miller went over the interview questions and answers with his superior. "Do we have enough to hold him?"

"No, let him leave. Ask him to remain available for the next two days. Ask him to advise us if he is called out of town on a job."

Miller returned to the office where Randy was waiting. "You may go for now, don't leave town without checking with us. Maybe you should get that lawyer to come in and see if we can work out some protection for you in exchange for testimony against Wong."

"Testify against Wong! Not a chance! "Randy hesitated and stayed seated, reluctant to leave.

"Did you have anything else to tell us Mr. Romanov?" Miller urged him to speak.

"I'll let you know tomorrow. I need time to sort all this out." Randy looked sideways.

Miller repeated his assurances. "We're here to protect you. If you

RON ROSEWOOD

can help us, that could help you too. You know how the system works."

Randy stood up and nodded slightly. He turned and slowly left the office. *He'll be back tomorrow.* Miller thought, as he completed a few notations in the file before putting it back in Rod's file cabinet.

ॐ

Rod arrived home in the late morning to Mrs. Sweeny buttering toast in the kitchen. She turned at the sound of Rod's footsteps. Seeing Rod's face she sensed the news was not good. "I was just making up some breakfast for Ann." She fished two eggs from the boiling water and put them in eggcups on the tray. She began picking up the tray.

Rod motioned her to put the tray back on the counter. "I have to speak with Ann. You can go home now, thank you for all your help"

Mrs. Sweeny paled. She remained silent but leaned in and gave Rod a hug, which he reciprocated. She gave him a slight smile patted him on the shoulder and left out the front door.

Rod walked towards the bedroom and lightly knocked on the door. "Ann, it's me... Are you awake? "

"I'm fixing my hair in the bathroom," she replied, "I'll be done in a minute."

Rod remained standing. This was not going to be easy. In his fifteen years as a policeman, he had informed families of deaths numerous times. This was different, this was their son. This was as close to the end of the world as any person could get. *What words could comfort a woman confronting these circumstances?*

Ann stepped out of the bathroom. She looked at Rod standing there with a sorrowful look on his face. She looked at the clock on the wall. She took two steps toward Rod and stopped, as if she had walked into an invisible barrier. "Oh my God, Chris is dead."

Rod could see Ann was straining to remain calm. "Yes, they found his body this morning. I'm so sorry Ann."

"No! This isn't happening, my baby, no!" Ann began sobbing

uncontrollably. Rod stepped forward in an attempt to hold her, but Ann turned her back towards him and fell to the floor.

"Don't come near me!" Ann screamed and raised both hands to cover her face. "This is your fault Rod, they warned you to stop working on the case. Why didn't you do something?"

"I'm sorry. I thought I did all I could to protect you and Chris." Rod whispered.

"Is that what you call your best? Look at us! Here we are with no son, no future and you're saying you did all you could. Why does this have to be us?" She sobbed." What has Chris done? What have we done? Why can't we have what everyone has? A real life. Why do we have to live in fear and uncertainty? Just leave me alone Rod, leave this room."

Rod left the room and sat down at the kitchen table. He began sobbing and let his head drop his forearms crossed on the table-top. He remembered the happy family moments he had shared with Chris and Ann. Their first Christmas, first house, Chris' school plays and bike lessons. Memories would be all they had to console them. Thirteen years condensed down to a handful of memories.

Rod was shocked out of deep thought by his ringing cell phone. "We'll be down in thirty minutes." He knocked on the bedroom door where Ann was curled up on the bed. "That was the hospital, they have Chris there. I'll go down and do the paperwork."

"I want to come. I have to come. I have to see him."

CHAPTER 51

Arriving at the hospital, and checking with admissions, Rod and Ann were directed to the morgue area.

The elevator was only a few feet down a hall off the waiting room. They rode down one floor and stepped through the opening elevator door. An orderly stood in silence beside a bed that held a sheet covered body. There was a single chair beside the lowered bed. Rod and Ann approached the middle of the bed. The doctor nodded to the attendant. He drew the sheet half way back and Rod nodded recognition. "Yes, that's our son." He put his left arm around Ann.

Ann gasped when she saw Chris. The finality of the moment struck her. Rod helped her sit on the chair beside the gurney. Reaching for her son's cold lifeless hand, she gazed in grief at his body. Chris' face still held the look of terror that he experienced. His face was ashen and blue. There was a restlessness about him that reflected outward as if he was trying to say to her, "Is this is my destiny?" She began weeping.

The attendant and the doctor, respecting their privacy, left the room. Ann sat there holding Chris's hand and stroking his hair. She gazed at the motionless shell of what had been a vibrant boy, now emptied of his robustness. Tears ran down her cheeks. She mourned for her son and friend. Time was meaningless. There was no longer any reason to be concerned with time. She sat there recalling the thirteen years of life that Chris had shared with her and Rod.

Twenty minutes later, Rod gently helped Ann to her feet. He turned her to face the doorway, while he replaced the white sheet over his son's body. *They will pay with their lives son, be assured of that!*

Rod spent the next six weeks readjusting to life. Life without Chris and life attending to Ann's health. He visited her daily at the institution, seeing very gradual improvement in her condition. Ann's prognosis was not encouraging, according to her doctors. They informed Rod that people who suffer from a nervous break-down and seek out treatment usually begin to recover within a few weeks time with the help of inpatient psychiatric treatment. Longer-term recovery was more unpredictable and could take years. In Ann's case, based on her previous mental health problems and her current condition, he suggested that the expected recovery period, if any, could be several years.

CHAPTER 52

Rod arrived at work to friendly waves and greetings from his fellow officers. He went directly to his prearranged appointment with Staff Sergeant Miller.

Staff Sergeant Miller greeted him with a handshake and a pat on the shoulder. "Welcome back Sergeant. Step in my and have a seat." Rod sat down on the chair facing Miller's desk. "We've made some progress on your cases. We have Maurice Romanov and Steffi Meyer charged with kidnapping and murder. The Crown Prosecutor is confident of a speedy trial and a certain conviction."

"I'm pleased to hear that, what about Randy Romanov, has he been charged?"

"Mr. Romanov was being investigated in connection with the hit on Lena Murin and Rex Trent. I doubt if we can succeed in prosecuting him on any of the murder cases. We had him agreeing to testify against Maurice or Steffi, in connection with the kidnapping case. Neither the Romanovs or Steffi still won't implicate Wong in the Lena Murin case."

Rod nodded. "That still leaves Wong clear, yet it was him who ordered the hits." He realized Miller's words were referring to the past tense. "What do you mean Randy *was* being investigated?"

"That could well be where we reached a dead end. As I said, Randy was the key and he was becoming more cooperative. We had had several talks with him. Before we could convince him to give anyone up, he was found dead in his suite. It's a pity we failed to get Randy to see it was in his interest to cooperate sooner."

"When did that happen?"

"Two weeks ago, we kept it from the press hoping to get some leads from the street."

"Was he murdered?"

"Inconclusive he was loaded with Cocaine, a massive overdose. He either, did it himself or someone encouraged him. Everything was there in the suite."

"This is why I am convinced there are powerful people like Wong pushing the buttons. What are we going to do now?"

"Rod, there is no *"we"* here, you are still off the case. You can see that, can't you?"

"In fact sir, the intended purpose of my appointment with you today was to tender my resignation." Rod reached in his inside breast pocket and handed Staff Sergeant Miller an envelope along with his badge.

Miller glanced down at the items Rod handed him. He took it without opening the envelope. They both knew how it read. "Sergeant, you are giving up a fifteen year career, are you sure a leave of absence might be a the way to proceed?"

"Quite sure sir. My hard work with the force has resulted in a complete disarray of my family, of my life. My son is dead, and my wife is quite likely permanently institutionalized, if I don't do this, it could be the end of me as well."

"I understand what you are saying Rod. However, I'll tell you what; I'll give you forty-eight hours before I turn this in. In the meantime if you wish to reconsider let me know. We can arrange to have you to speak with a psychologist"

"I won't be reconsidering Sir, but I do appreciate your suggestion." Rod held out his hand and gave Miller a firm handshake. "Let me know when the paperwork is finalized and I will slip over and attend to it."

Rod felt as though a huge burden had lifted from his shoulders. He stepped out into the morning sunshine. The crows were scolding everything that moved, the traffic noise was steady, and the warming waves of hot air wafted up from the pavement as he made his way to his car.

He had a plan. A plan that would take a few months to implement; However, what are a few months compared to half a lifetime? In the meantime, there were fish to be caught.

CHAPTER 53
Six Months Later

It was late January. Rod booked a trip to Atlantic City for two weeks at the Trump Tower and Casino. He told the hotel manager that he was there to do some research and writing for his novel and did not want to be interrupted. The next morning, he rented a car and drove to Miami where he took a mini cruise to Nassau. He decided to stay over for the night and booked into a fourth floor room at the Sheraton Nassau Hotel & Casino under the name Don Martin. He had learned from enquiries and other contacts that Steven Lee Wong was vacationing here in Nassau for two weeks.

With tinted glasses and Clint Eastwood stubble, Rod roamed the city freely. It was mid-evening when he spotted Wong in the Telegraph Bar chatting up a stunning dark haired woman in her mid-twenties. Walking past the bar entrance, he loitered in front of a newsstand, thumbing through a copy of Business Week. Rod walked over to the cashier and paid for the magazine in U.S. currency. He walked a few steps to a seat about thirty feet from the bar entrance. In about twenty minutes he saw the woman leave the bar, walking hastily toward the elevator.

Rod latched on to a crowd of people walking behind her towards the elevator. The elevator stopped and three couples came out. Rod and the other five people got in and started up. The woman stepped out at the eleventh floor, along with another couple. Rod hung back and then came out a few seconds later. He glanced to the left and saw the woman entering room 1115. Rod slipped into the ice dispensing room almost directly across from her room. He picked up an ice bucket and began feeding quarters into the vending machine. He was almost through filling it when he saw Wong sauntering toward the room. No one else was in sight.

With his body slightly turned, Rod called over in a pleasant voice. "Pardon me sir, would you have change for a dollar? This machine just ate my last quarter." He chuckled.

Wong stepped toward Rod, fishing for change in his jacket pocket. "Yes, I may just have some," he replied as he withdrew a handful of change. He looked down and picked out four quarters. "Here you are." Wong reached out with his right hand.

Rod reached out with his left hand and grabbed Wong's right wrist, yanking him out of the hallway into the vending room. Before Wong could regain his balance, Rod was thrusting forward with his right hand from down low. The knife sank easily into Wong's upper belly continuing up into his vital organs. "Welcome to Nassau, Stevie boy."

Wong's eyes popped opened wide in terror. He recognized Rod, "You," was all he could utter before slumping forward.

"Thanks for the change," Rod whispered, as he twisted the hilt of the knife, drew it back and then thrust it forward again. "How does this feel, Stevie boy?" He thrust the knife forward again. "Are you enjoying life?" Thrusting. "This one is on me! " Thrusting. "Will your kids miss you?" Rod gave the knife a final thrust and twist. "There you go Bastard!" He moved back and Wong collapsed in a heap on the floor.

After, wiping the knife on the jacket of Wong's collapsed body, Rod, stepped back. Inspecting his own clothes for any signs of blood on his dark pants and black shirt. He slipped the knife into his inside blazer jacket pocket strolled down the hall to the elevator, he pressed the second floor and exited the final level to the lobby via the stairs.

Rod went in to the Telegraph Bar and ordered a two shots of Hennigan's on ice. He took two sips of the scotch, got up and walked to the washroom. He carefully wiped the fish filleting knife clean of prints stuffed the knife into a planter box beside the door.

Going back to the bar, he sat down and finished his beer. Rod was just getting up to leave when a police cruiser and an ambulance arrived simultaneously.

"I wonder, what's that about?" Rod commented to the bartender.

"He probably had a heart attack from too much excitement, if you know what I mean." The barman winked and smiled as he wiped the bar in front of Rod. "It happens all the time."

"Some guys have all the fun," Rod grinned, "Pour me another, and hey, have one for yourself."

"Why not, it's still early. By the way, will you be golfing ? We have a fine course here, just for our guests."

"I love to golf and I do have a few days to spare as I've finished my work here before schedule."

"What do you do? No let me guess. Judging by your dark clothes, I'd say you're an undertaker, you bury them. Am I right?"

"Pretty close, my friend. I do it on paper. I write crime novels?" Rod smiled at the nearness of the barman's guess.

"Will you write me into your next novel, my name is Jake, my girlfriend would go wild over something like that!"

"Sure, why not." Rod stood up. "Have a good evening Jake and thanks for the chit chat. I may see you tomorrow."

"Sleep tight now."

The next day Rod took the mini cruise boat back to Miami.

CHAPTER 54

Len and Rod sat at the sports bar watching the NHL playoffs, the pregame show was finishing. "Who do you like?" Len asked.

"Vancouver, all the way? How about you, Len, will it be Vancouver or Boston?"

"I think the East was better all season. Boston should do it with their tough play. You know what they say Rod, good guys always finish last."

"That depends on what game you happen to be playing." Rod winked at Len and raised his glass. "Down with the bad guys."

"Said like a true cop."

"Retired cop, Len, retired! By the way, how is your novel on the Murin drowning coming along?"

"The husband did it." Len grinned "Not very original is it?"

"He had an alibi, he was several hours away!"

"True, he was, but he spiked her one quarter bottle of wine with an eye clearing medication."

"I see, so she drank that?"

"You bet, it made her have a heart attack, she died instantly. Furthermore the pool chlorine disguised the medication."

"And so the husband managed to pull off a perfect murder?"

"It happens," Len winked at Rod, "By the way I'm sending a copy of the novel to Sergeant Jones in Calgary."

"He may find it interesting indeed. So what is your next book about?"

"I thought I would write about the Lena Murin unsolved case."

"Good luck with that Lennie! I've been there. I don't need a copy of that."

"Why not? I'll pencil in a surprise ending." Len winked again at Rod. Rod smiled back "Perhaps I can help you with that!"

The End

AUTHOR BIOGRAPHY

RON ROSEWOOD is a Canadian author who has affection for the outdoors and adventures found there.

He was raised and educated in Saskatchewan, Canada and practiced his accounting profession in British Columbia. He is retired and currently resides on Vancouver Island, B.C.

Ron is a Professional Author Member of the Crime Writers of Canada, the Federation of B.C. Writers, the Romance Writers of America, as well as an active Senior member of The Cowichan Writers Group.

Previously he had several stories appear in *Blood Moon Rising Magazine* and *Werewolf Magazine* both published in New York. He was also featured in articles appearing in *B. C. Seniors Magazine* as well as the *Cowichan Leader Pictorial News*.

OTHER BOOKS WRITTEN BY RON ROSEWOOD INCLUDE

Melissa's Wish List
an Adventure Romance

Postdated Romance
a Paranormal Romance

From Hilarious to Outrageous
an Anthology of Short Stories

Werewolves Amongst Us
a crime/suspense novelette

The Chosen Twin
a combination of personal challenges, suspense and romance

Ron can be reached by e-mail at
ronrosewood@yahoo.ca